"Katie, go back in

A car suddenly careened into view, driving right up onto the sidewalk. In a matter of moments it would plow right into them. Brayden drew his gun and fired into the windshield, but the car didn't slow. He spun to the side and fell, rolling several times before he smacked into the brick side of the store.

Brayden scrambled to his feet. The car was empty now, front end mashed from the impact...and Katie was gone.

Ella sprinted to the fenced alley between the shop and the building next to it. The K-9 must be following Katie. He took off in pursuit. As he, too, rounded the corner, he saw Ella chasing them, Katie a few steps ahead of the man who had taken her. She turned to look back, eyes huge with fear.

"Stop! Alaska State Trooper!" Brayden yelled.

ALASKA K-9 UNIT

*These state troopers fight for justice
with the help of their brave canine partners.*

Dana Mentink is a nationally bestselling author. She has been honored to win two Carol Awards, a HOLT Medallion and an RT Reviewers' Choice Best Book Award. She's authored more than thirty novels to date for Love Inspired Suspense and Harlequin Heartwarming. Dana loves feedback from her readers. Contact her at danamentink.com.

Visit the Author Profile page at Harlequin.com for more titles.

YUKON JUSTICE

DANA MENTINK

LOVE INSPIRED SUSPENSE
INSPIRATIONAL ROMANCE

If you purchased this book without a cover you should be aware that this book is stolen property. It was reported as "unsold and destroyed" to the publisher, and neither the author nor the publisher has received any payment for this "stripped book."

Special thanks and acknowledgment are given to Dana Mentink for her contribution to the Alaska K-9 Unit miniseries.

LOVE INSPIRED® SUSPENSE

INSPIRATIONAL ROMANCE

Recycling programs for this product may not exist in your area.

ISBN-13: 978-1-335-72269-0

Yukon Justice

Copyright © 2021 by Harlequin Books S.A.

All rights reserved. No part of this book may be used or reproduced in any manner whatsoever without written permission except in the case of brief quotations embodied in critical articles and reviews.

This is a work of fiction. Names, characters, places and incidents are either the product of the author's imagination or are used fictitiously. Any resemblance to actual persons, living or dead, businesses, companies, events or locales is entirely coincidental.

This edition published by arrangement with Harlequin Books S.A.

For questions and comments about the quality of this book, please contact us at CustomerService@Harlequin.com.

Love Inspired
22 Adelaide St. West, 40th Floor
Toronto, Ontario M5H 4E3, Canada
www.Harlequin.com

Printed in U.S.A.

What shall we then say to these things?
If God be for us, who can be against us?
—*Romans* 8:31

To those first responders and their families.
Thank you for being the hands and feet of Jesus.

ONE

The young reindeer nuzzled Katie Kapowski's palm with velvet lips, pawing the ground uneasily as nighttime settled around them. The animal was too thin, with an Alaskan winter closing in.

"It's okay, Sweetie. We'll get your mama back." Anger at Uncle Terrence burned in her stomach. The baby reindeer was suffering since Terrence had stolen his mother, Lulu, from the Family K Reindeer Ranch. At least the rest of the small herd had kept a close eye on Sweetie. Reindeer, above all else, were a family-oriented species. People should be so devoted.

Katie felt her own quiver of uncertainty at her return to the ranch. The job she'd left behind for a week pulled at her, assistant to Alaska K-9 Unit Colonel Lorenza Gallo and the group of elite state troopers along with their highly trained dogs. How hard she'd worked to get there. She was accustomed to the sleek Anchorage office, her multiple computer screens and a constant bustle of activity. But now she'd exchanged her stylish slacks and low heels for jeans and grimy work boots, auburn hair caught in a hurried ponytail. No professional polish required on a ranch near Palmer, Alaska, a town of barely seven thousand people, thirty-seven miles from the K-9 unit headquarters.

Goose bumps prickled along her neck. She whirled around. Nothing was there, only a twig borne by the autumn wind. The ranch was a broad sweep of flat pasture that lost itself into the neighbor's forested property to the west. The Frontier River defined the eastern property line. Isolated and wild. The quiet made her jumpy. The older animals shifted, intricate antlers highlighted by the setting sun. Reindeer were the only members of the deer species where the females sported antlers as well as the males. "Girl power," she whispered to a nearby female. "Wear those antlers proudly."

Katie stroked the baby reindeer's wiry fur in an effort to soothe them both. Was the animal also hearing noises? Or perhaps he was uneasy about the recent abduction. Three of the precious rescued animals had been stolen over the last few months. The Alaska K-9 team had recovered one, but Thunder, the male, and

Sweetie's mom, Lulu, were still missing. Katie's worry grew every day that they were not found.

Why steal reindeer to get back at Aunt Addie? It was still so hard to believe the culprit was her own uncle. Katie hadn't even known of Terrence's existence until the K-9 team found DNA that proved the perpetrator was a relative. Aunt Addie had no choice then but to come clean about her estranged brother. Still, stealing reindeer to punish his sister for some perceived slight? Could someone really be so juvenile? None of it made any sense to Katie.

Oh, Aunt Addie. Why couldn't you have told me sooner? she thought. Things with her aunt hadn't exactly gone smoothly since Katie's temporary return. Her aunt was still the same surly, stubborn woman who'd raised her from the age of ten, even less likely to filter her comments now that she was approaching sixty. Tact and finesse were unknown concepts in Addie's world.

"No one tells me how to run my ranch," she'd said. "I'm not changing a single thing, even if my brother has turned up to harass me. He's a cruel-hearted louse. Always has been."

Addie was doubly stressed with Terrence bent on not only ruining the ranch but also sabotaging the annual Christmas Fair looming in two months. So, yes, Katie knew her aunt had good reason to be short-tempered. But it didn't help that her outbursts had caused both her regular ranch hands to quit. Blaze was no loss, since he'd been stealing petty cash, but Gary had been a steady worker who'd endured one tongue-lashing too many from Addie. Now, with virtually no help, two hundred and fifty acres of Alaskan wilderness and a herd of twenty-three rescued reindeer to tend to, things were getting downright desperate.

Which meant, whether her aunt wanted to admit it or not, she needed Katie's help. Perhaps she could set a few things in order during her week away from the office without a major blowup with Aunt Addie.

A leaf scuffled over the top of hcr muddy boots, startling her. Her sideways movement subsequently alarmed Sweetie, who edged back to the comfort of his reindeer sisters.

Relax, Katie, she told herself. Addie was back at the main house. Law enforcement drove by on regular checks of the property, including Trooper Brayden Ford. An image of him popped into her mind along with the ever-present tension. Ridiculous. It didn't matter now that he'd almost cost her a position with the Alaska K-9 Unit in their Anchorage office. And, certainly, he must know she had not meant to humiliate him when she told him the truth about his girlfriend Jamie, though it proved mortifying. Water under the proverbial bridge, right? Still, she wished it was anyone but him patrolling her aunt's ranch at the moment.

Her eyes drifted upward. The October moon hung low in the inky sky and she sighed appreciatively as she breathed in the cold, scented with the musk of the animals gathered in the pasture pen and the meager remnants of the willow leaves they'd finished devouring. The lighter fur of their chests glimmered against the darkness. So quiet here, so peaceful, except for the ever-present drone of the mosquitoes. Nights like these made it hard to imagine why anybody, even Addie's disgruntled brother, would want to harm the ranch.

Why such covetousness over a place that existed purely to care for rescued reindeer? The ranch barely covered expenses, let alone made a profit. Not exactly a money factory. She said a quiet good-night to the animals. The gate squealed as she closed and secured the holding pen.

Something snapped in the distance. She tensed.

If Terrence was still bent on ruining the Family K, maybe he wasn't deterred by the trooper's attention. But the noise could have been anything, a rock tumbling from the bank into the Frontier River, a moose foraging for a snack, an elk, a bear… It was certainly *not* her uncle. She would spot him coming from way off since there was no cover to speak of.

Her phone pinged with an incoming call. Startled, she thumbed it on. "Hello?"

"It's really dark out here." The voice was a deep baritone.

She swatted a mosquito trying to settle on her windbreaker. "Very." Picturing Brayden and his big Newfoundland dog, Ella, made her sag with relief. She was grateful he had not witnessed her panicky behavior. It probably made her seem even more like a kid than the freckles splashed across her nose. And she certainly didn't want to give him any more reason to think her less than competent.

"Finishing up my security check," he said. "Everything's okay except Ella ate the bologna sandwich I was saving for dinner."

She could not restrain a smile. Ella, his highly trained underwater search-and-rescue canine, was a menace to all unsecured food items. She was grateful that Brayden and the other K-9 team members had been trying to help unearth the ranch saboteur. They had plenty on their hands already, including hunting down the murderous groom and best man who had framed the would-be bride, Violet James, who was currently in hiding to protect her unborn baby. With such an important case to tend to, she was doubly grateful that Brayden was checking up occasionally. Still, it would be easier if it was another officer, *any* other officer. Maybe she wouldn't feel so hesitant around someone else. There was just too much distrust between them. Still, though, the man needed a meal, and as Katie's mother used to say, "Anyone in my vicinity won't leave hungry unless they want to."

"Sorry about your dinner, Brayden. If you come by the main house, I'll fix you a peanut butter and jelly sandwich."

He sighed. "I guess I can't hope for bologna from a vegetarian."

"No, but I can offer some amazing tofu if you'd rather, with garlic and spices. You won't even miss the meat." She could not resist the gibe.

"I'll stick with the PB and J."

She was about to respond when several of the reindeer twitched, then bolted to the far side of the pen to huddle together. All of them were stiff with anxiety, ears pricked. They'd heard something she hadn't. But how could she explain it to Brayden without sounding like a scared kid? Bad enough she was twenty-four to his thirty-two and the one who had thrown the spotlight on his fickle girlfriend. It was *not* the time to add paranoia to that list. She must have remained silent for a beat too long.

"What's wrong, Katie?" he asked, suddenly stone-cold serious.

"I'm not sure. I'm near the pasture pen. I thought I heard something…" But there was nothing in the moonlight except the sprawling flatland, stubbled with wild grasses and the occasional clump of fireweed. "It's quiet now. It must have been my imagination."

He was all business now. "I'm driving down the river access road. I'll meet you at the gate."

"But there's probably no reason to—" Her sentence was cut short by distant shouting, followed by a shrill scream.

"The dock," she blurted into the phone. "It's Aunt Addie!"

"I'm on my way."

She kept the connection active, racing out of the pasture gate and securing the complicated latch system behind her with shaking fingers. Addie had been working on her computer in the main house not a half hour ago. Yet the scream had originated from the dock that jutted over the Frontier River. Had her aunt been out for a walk and fallen? Or was it something more sinister?

Katie's feet pounded as she charged across the grass and over the dirt access road, avoiding the mud as best she could. No sign of Brayden's vehicle yet. Another scream.

She shouted into the phone, "Addie's in trouble, Brayden. Help!"

Not waiting for an answer, she raced on. Grit from the road ground under the soles of her mud boots. The dock finally came into sight. She caught her aunt's silhouette, the sheen of her silvered brown hair glinting in the gloom. One slender arm was outstretched as if she was trying to ward off a blow, but there wasn't anyone else there, as far as Katie could see. She thought she heard a pop over the roar of the water. *A gunshot?* Addie jerked as if she'd been struck and toppled backward off the dock.

Instinct overrode all other inputs. Heedless of anything except saving her aunt, Katie made it to the edge in three strides and dived in feet-first. She had grown up on the ranch since her parents were killed. She knew every inch of the place, especially the riverbed. This offshoot of the Frontier River that branched and meandered shallowly in most places was deep near the dock.

And *frigid* with snowmelt from the surrounding Chugach Mountains no matter what the season.

On impact, the freezing water stripped her of breath and turned her muscles into knots as she sank. The heavy boots she'd been wearing immediately filled with water and became anchors that dragged her toward the bottom. Why hadn't she thought to shake them off before she'd jumped in?

Gasping in shock, she fought off momentary paralysis. She freed her feet from the boots, kicked hard and propelled herself to the surface. Dashing the water from her eyes, she turned in a tight circle. There was no sign of her aunt anywhere. Nor was there anyone else. Had she imagined the gunshot? Panic roiled through her. Addie was tough as nails but she was small-framed, like Katie, and had been recovering from bronchitis, which had sapped her normal energy. The river could suck her away and snuff out her life in a matter of moments.

"Aunt Addie!" she shouted, treading water. Her arms were already numb and she was beginning to lose feeling in her legs. Flying insects danced across the choppy surface as the dark eddies of water rolled and curled over themselves. She felt a presence on the dock. Hope sparked inside her... It must be Brayden and Ella. She opened her mouth to call out to them until she realized her grave mistake.

It wasn't Brayden. A figure stepped clear of

the shadows for the first time. She recognized the body type, long and lean, the slightly bow-legged stance so like her aunt's.

Her long-lost uncle, Terrence Kapowski.

Then her brain registered the other fact. He was holding a gun.

The sound she'd heard had indeed been a bullet, aimed at her aunt.

"Uncle Terrence," she yelled. "I'm Katie, your niece. Please…" Her request trailed off.

Terrence's expression was blank in the eerie light, but his steady grip on the pistol did not waver.

It was dreamlike, her uncle standing there against the pewter sky, the gun pointed at her, a small and deadly circle of gray. She saw more of the family resemblance visible in the determined line of his jaw, the narrow chin so like her aunt's.

So like her own.

"Uncle Terrence," she shouted again.

He cocked his head as if the sound of his name confused him. "You think you're going to get it?"

"Get what?" she asked, teeth chattering.

"The ranch. You can't have it. Not Addie, not you. I'm their only son."

"No one wants to take anything from you," she tried telling him.

"And no one will." He took a step closer. "I'll see you both dead first."

Her brain could still hardly process the facts. Terrence had been trying to kill Addie, who was now lost in the water, perhaps already dead.

Now he meant to do the same to her.

She watched helplessly as he took aim, ready for the kill.

Brayden was out of the vehicle and running for the dock. Ella lumbered after him, black fur blending with the gloom as the last remnants of sunlight surrendered. There was a man on the dock whom he recognized from the photos. Terrence Kapowski. Terrence immediately sprinted for the bushes.

"State trooper," Brayden shouted. "Stop or I'll shoot." The man skidded down the bank, vanishing into the darkness. Ella barked furiously, her deep woof echoing across the water.

"Brayden!" The scream was barely audible over Ella's racket and the sound of the rushing water.

He raced to the edge of the dock. Frantically he scanned the river for any sign of Katie or Addie. "Katie," he thundered. "Where are you?"

Katie's head bobbed up to the surface, her face a pale glimmer in the tumult. "My aunt's been shot."

Again he scanned behind him, under the dock, along the bank. Had Terrence found a hiding place, waiting to unleash more gunfire? Control the shooter or get the women out of the water? Muttering a prayer that he was making the right choice, he stripped off his gun belt and cell phone. Ella was already dancing in eagerness on the edge of the dock.

"Find," he told her. She would normally do her job from the bank or the deck of a boat, but nothing about this was normal. Addie, he prayed, was still alive. If she was, Ella would find her. The K-9 charged off the edge of the dock, cannonballing into the river. Brayden followed suit.

The cold slammed into him as he hit the surface feetfirst. He swam immediately to Katie.

"I'm okay," she said, waving him off. "We have to find Addie."

But she was shuddering with cold, her lips dark, which meant the onset of hypothermia could be moments away. He grasped her forearm. "Get out of the water. Ella will locate Addie."

She ignored him. "I know this river. It will carry her toward the far bank. She's unconscious. We don't have time." She pulled away and swam farther out.

"Katie," he started.

"I have to find her." Katie's tone was laced with panic.

A splash from several feet away jerked their attention. He exhaled in relief. Ella had indeed found Addie. "Good girl, El. Bring her to shore."

Wasted breath. Ella knew what to do. She always did.

Katie started toward her aunt, but Brayden stopped her. "Trust the dog. We need to get you out right away."

Addie was floating on her back, eyes closed. Ella grabbed her by her shirt collar and began towing her toward the bank. Addie's weight was no match for the muscular Newfie. The dog's webbed paws cleaved the water effortlessly. He turned his attention back to Katie, but her eyes were riveted to her aunt. Before he could offer any assistance, she was swimming hard toward shore.

He followed suit, scanning for any sign that Terrence might still be lying in wait. He'd radioed for an ambulance and his fellow troopers as soon as he'd heard the first gunshot. Two were close by—they'd already be en route along with the local cops—but it would take a good thirty minutes for anyone else to get there from their Anchorage base. The ambulance would arrive much sooner, he hoped.

Brayden slogged out of the water at the graveled portion of the bank where Ella had deposited Addie and begun to lick her face. Katie dropped to her knees and put her cheek next to her aunt's mouth.

The look she turned on Brayden made his stomach drop.

"She's not breathing," Katie whispered.

"Ella, watch," he said. The big dog shook the water from her thick coat and sat up, nose twitching as she sampled the air. She was not an attack dog, but if Terrence tried to get close again, Brayden felt confident she would alert him with a bark. It was that same bark that proved maddening at three in the morning, but now he was grateful for it.

Katie had already started rescue breathing, thanks to the training Colonel Gallo insisted every member of the department receive. He took over. "Try to find the bullet wound and stop the bleeding."

After a quick exam, Katie stripped off her jacket and pressed it to her aunt's shoulder.

He clasped his hands together and began to administer compressions, alternating with respirations.

After several cycles, they stopped to assess. Addie remained cold and lifeless.

"Come on, come on," he whispered. "Breathe."

Were they going to lose her? Katie's distraught expression told him she was entertaining the same horrible thought.

He started in on another round of CPR.

But Addie's chest remained still as the Alaskan night.

"Aunt Addie," Katie entreated. "Please don't leave me."

He added his silent plea to hers as he launched into more compressions.

TWO

Brayden's arms flexed in regular motion as he kept up the compressions for another series. Water poured from Addie's mouth until her lungs cleared.

Katie's limbs were rubber and she was trembling badly as she sought a pulse. "I'm not sure. I'm shaking too much."

Brayden checked Addie's neck. The seconds rolled by in torturous slow motion. "I got it," he said. "A heartbeat."

With a flutter of hope, Katie put her check to her aunt's lips. "She's breathing."

They watched and monitored with painful attention while she maintained the pressure on her aunt's bullet wound. Brayden left just long enough to retrieve a pair of blankets from his vehicle, one to put over Addie and another that he draped over Katie's shoulders. They huddled there shivering, eyes fixed on the woman, until the ambulance arrived and a cop directed the medics to take over.

Katie noticed two other officers who arrived on scene. Troopers Poppy Walsh and Helena Maddox quickly listened to Brayden's rundown, their two dogs tense with anticipation. Ella greeted her canine coworkers with an enthusiastic tail wag.

"We'll see if we can track Terrence," Poppy said, snapping a long leash on her Irish wolfhound. "I'll check the riverbank."

Brayden spoke through chattering teeth. "Not alone."

Helena flashed a smile. "Nope. Luna and I have her back." Helena patted the sleek Norwegian elkhound sitting obediently at her side.

"So I don't need to tell you to exercise extreme caution?" he said.

"Affirmative," Helena retorted in a sassy tone. "You don't."

"There's a section of the bank where the water runs shallow," Katie said. "It forms sort of a cave. There are a couple places like that where he could be hiding. Please... I know Brayden doesn't have to say it, but I do. Be careful. My uncle..." It almost hurt to call him that. "He would have murdered us."

Both women nodded. "Take care of your aunt," Poppy told her. "We'll report if we find anything." She glanced at the horizon. "There's a storm rolling in, so we'd better be quick."

Katie watched Addie being eased onto a stretcher and loaded into the ambulance. The adrenaline was beginning to pass, leaving her in a daze. It was unreal, what had just happened. *Sickening.* Her kin, her family member, had tried to kill her. She went dizzy with the shock of it.

Brayden took her hand. "Let's get you into the car. We'll stop at the house and you can put on some dry clothes before I drive you to the hospital."

The hospital. Of course that was where they would be going next. Because Addie had been shot. Would she die? Through a haze, she saw Ella stand and shake water from her voluminous coat. On impulse, she knelt and cradled the dog's enormous head in her hands. "Thank you, Ella, for rescuing my aunt."

The K-9 licked at a strand of Katie's sodden hair.

She turned to Brayden. "And thank you, too."

Brayden shrugged. "Ella did the real work. She loves any excuse to get in the water. Come on now."

He opened the rear door of his SUV for Ella and the front for Katie. Then he handed her his coat to throw around her since the blanket was soggy, an Alaska State Trooper emblem emblazoned on the front. "D-don't you need it?" she asked.

"I'll change into a dry uniform at the house." He cranked up the heat. "Besides, I'm very rough and tough and manly and all that. My blood is naturally warm," he managed through chattering teeth.

Amazingly, she felt her mouth curl into a smile, and a tiny laugh escaped—a giggle, of all things. "Of course. I should have realized that."

Quiet settled between them as he drove. The blackness of the night seemed to swallow everything until they pulled up the graveled drive of the house. Hurriedly, she raced to the guest room and threw on another set of clothes, a windbreaker and tennis shoes. She found Brayden emerging from the downstairs bathroom in a dry uniform.

"Ready?"

Was she? She swallowed the panic and nodded.

Back on the road, she wondered what they would find at the hospital. She relived the pop of the gunshot, her aunt's scream, the weapon aimed at her forehead. It came back to her like a sledgehammer blow. Aunt Addie had been *shot* and might not survive. In one moment, Katie's life might be stripped of the woman who had taken her in after the death of her parents. That had been completely unexpected, too. One moment they were alive and the next they were gone. If Aunt Addie died, Katie would be all alone in the world.

Without warning, she was sobbing, tears running in rivulets down her cheeks. Gulping in deep breaths, she tried to stem the tide, but she could do nothing but wrap her arms around herself and cry, wishing the darkness would swallow her up.

She felt the car slowing, and the next thing she knew, Brayden had pulled off the road and stopped. He went around to the passenger side and opened the door, unbuckling her seat belt and pulling her into his arms. His skin was warm now, his spare clothes smelling of a recent laundering.

She detested being like this in front of him. It was humiliating to be so out of control, yet she simply could not stop. Choking gasps escaped her and she cried, "I don't want to lose her like my parents." The words bubbled out in a rush of misery. The old wound had torn open again, unleashing fresh agony.

Brayden hugged her close and pressed his cheek to the top of her head. "It's going to be okay." And to her surprise, he said a gentle prayer, asking God to intercede for Addie and for Katie's own peace and protection. Her anxiety diminished and soon she was able to breathe regularly. She pressed her face against his broad chest, delaying the inevitable rush of embarrassment that was sure to follow. Just for a moment, she allowed herself to accept the comfort he offered, the relief from her terror of the "what-ifs."

He moved her to arm's length. His green gaze peered at her so intently, her face flushed hot. Here she was, crying like an overwrought child all over Brayden Ford. And hadn't he voted during her oral board examination to "not hire" her because he found her too young, too inexperienced for this line of work, too...*emotional*, as she'd accidentally seen on the note sheet? If Lorenza Gallo hadn't overridden his no vote, she would never have gotten the job.

She straightened and swiped at her eyes with the back of her hand. "I'm sorry. How embarrassing."

He didn't smile. "Not embarrassing. *Human.* You're afraid for your aunt. You've just been through something awful."

She cleared her throat and tried to push the sodden hair away that had escaped the ponytail, but her fingers wouldn't cooperate.

Gently, he reached out and smoothed the strand for her, tucking it behind her ear.

"There," he said. "Picture-perfect."

Perfect. That was a good one. She hiccuped, looked away, fiddled with her jacket. "I'm okay now. Can we keep going?"

"Of course," he said, guiding her back to the vehicle, where Ella still snoozed in the back seat.

Cheeks still burning, she tried to explain. "My parents were killed in a wreck when I was ten, along with my unborn brother. I came to live with Addie on the Family K, which I am sure was not what either one of us wanted." The words would not stop spilling out. "She was strict, brusque and no-nonsense, and it took me such a long time to get used to it. My mom was the exact opposite, warm and charming. She made me little notes in my lunch bag and drew faces on my bananas." She swallowed hard at the memory.

Surprisingly, he looked genuinely interested. "So Aunt Addie had big shoes to fill?"

Katie sighed. "Addie never signed up to be my mother, or anyone else's, but she sacrificed for me, did the best she could. I remember she helped me finish a fourth-grade project about reindeer. There was a parent-night presentation and I had no one to bring, of course. My aunt not only came, but she trailered a reindeer to the school parking lot for a sort of show-and-tell. The kids were wowed." She felt tears threaten again. "When I think that she might not make it…"

He reached over and squeezed her hand. "One thing I've learned in this business, Katie, is that nothing is over until God says it is."

That surprised her. "Anyway, thank you." She tugged at her necklace, trying to still her nerves. Twisting the enameled pendant always calmed her and she was relieved it hadn't come loose in the river.

"I recognize that flower," he said, pointing to her pendant. "I've seen it before."

"It's a forget-me-not, a Christmas gift from my mother. I never take it off."

"Alaska state flower, right?"

"Right."

"I earned a wilderness merit badge in Scouts, you know," he said with mock pride. "I know my way around wildflowers."

His cheeky grin lightened her spirit, as she figured he'd intended to do. She'd not seen this side of him and probably never would again. Extreme circumstances and all that, the same reason she was babbling her life story.

When they pulled into the parking lot, Brayden's phone rang. He answered. After a moment, he fell silent, listening intently before he thanked the caller. He disconnected.

She didn't have to ask if it was good news or bad. His frown said it all.

"Terrence got away," he said. "Storm's coming in tonight, so they'll work the area tomorrow after it has passed to see if they missed anything."

"Maybe he's gone. He might have decided to leave town." The words rang false even to her own ears.

"I'll see you both dead first."

Remembering his angry expression when he'd pulled the trigger, she knew he wasn't going anywhere until he got what he came for.

Brayden tapped his pencil on the notepad in front of him in the briefing room of the Anchorage-based K-9 team headquarters. He hadn't realized his fingers had been working on a project of their own until Hunter McCord nudged him in the ribs, his smile impish. "Stick with your day job."

"What?"

Hunter pointed. "You'll never make it as an artist. I did better drawings in preschool."

"Funny." He hadn't realized he'd been doodling a picture of a flower, and he noted with a start that it was a forget-me-not. Why was the state flower of Alaska on his mind?

Hunter fixed him with a blue-eyed stare. "Thinking about someone?"

"No," he said hurriedly. Hunter, above all people, should know Brayden wasn't seeing anyone since Jamie had shredded his heart. Hunter's own cop father had been killed by a shady girlfriend, and it had helped Brayden to know that he wasn't the only one blinded by love, or what he thought was love.

He remembered Katie's tentative smile. *"It's a forget-me-not, a Christmas gift from my mother. I never take it off."* Funny. That constant twiddling, the nervous pacing, had given him the impression during that oral board interview eight months before that Katie was not sure of herself. But he'd been right then, to "not recommend" her during that interview, hadn't he? Others were more qualified, more seasoned in police procedure. His skin went clammy at the memory of what had happened three months after that...how she'd told him what he didn't want to hear about Jamie.

"Is this your way of getting back at me for not recommending your hire?" he'd demanded. *"You'd make stuff up about my girlfriend?"*

He still remembered the scarlet flush that instantly colored her face. Maybe it was the same hue that colored his when he realized later that she'd been telling him the truth.

"The doctors are confident that Addie Kapowski will recover."

He snapped back in time to hear his boss, Colonel Lorenza Gallo, finish with, "Katie is taking on the running of the ranch until her aunt can return."

Trooper Sean West grinned suddenly. "Plenty of reindeer in Nome, if Katie wants to add to the herd. They prefer the road to the tundra when it snows, and man, can they block the highway."

There was a ripple of laughter.

Lorenza continued. "I granted her request to extend her time off to an official leave of absence. I know we're stretched thin right now, so I'm making some private arrangements to ensure her safety. But I want to assign one of you as full-time point person on the Terrence Kapowski case." The colonel's silver coiffure was perfect, her posture tall and erect as she stared at him. "Brayden, that's you."

He blinked. "Me? I don't think…"

"Poppy and Maya are knee-deep in finding the Seavers."

The Seavers were a survivalist family proving hard to locate. Their team tech guru, Eli Partridge, was committed to finding them, particularly since it was his dying godmother's last wish. Brayden himself had found a trace of the off-grid family's presence in a cabin in the Chugach State Park, but the trail had ended there.

"And Gabriel's got a lead on Violet James," Lorenza added. "Time's getting short since she is approaching her due date. We've got people working multiple assignments and you're already on the Kapowski case since you and Ella were on scene last night. So, yes, I'm assigning you." Her eyebrow arched. "Unless you have some sort of compelling reason to refuse?"

Compelling reason? Only that he could hardly bear to look Katie in the face, and she no doubt felt the same. And the fact that she was as close to his boss as a granddaughter. Sighing, he scrubbed a hand across his jaw. And he was sure there were plenty other great reasons to stay far away from Katie that he could not bring to mind at the moment. "No, ma'am," he heard himself say. "I have no reason to refuse."

The colonel smiled a cat-in-the-cream grin. "That's what I thought. We can smooth out the details later." She turned to Gabriel, whose Saint Bernard sprawled at his feet. "Report on Wells and Dennis?"

Everyone perked up. Lance Wells and Jared Dennis were wanted in the murder of a tour guide and the attempted murder of bride-to-be Violet James, the pregnant woman who was now in hiding. The stakes were high and the thought of having Wells so close to Violet made everyone's pulse beat faster.

"Nothing new. Last sighting was in Anchorage, as you know," Gabriel said. "Worrying, since Violet was spotted here, too."

"Probably going for prenatal care, but we haven't been able to nail down where yet," Helena interjected.

Gabriel's mouth tightened. "We need to get Violet home safe and sound by Thanksgiving."

"I second that, since my darling fiancée has it in her heart for Violet to be her maid of honor at our Christmas wedding." Hunter smiled. "What's a wedding without your best friend?"

They did a round-robin sharing and discussed next steps. Brayden felt both frustrated and bewildered that he was now assigned full-time to the Terrence Kapowski case. Was he being diverted from the main action? Or especially trusted with someone who meant the world to the colonel? When the meeting wrapped, he slugged down a cup of coffee, which he managed to drip on his shirt before he popped into Lorenza's office.

She glanced at him over the top of her reading glasses. "You're wearing your coffee."

"Er, yes, Colonel. Sorry. Um, I wondered what you meant by private arrangements to protect Katie."

"I would have been disappointed if you hadn't come to ask, but before I get to that, let's just clear the air here. You don't want to work with Katie because she found out you didn't recommend her for the job. What's more, she tried to warn you about the woman you were dating, whom you ultimately wound up arresting, leaving you ashamed and humiliated."

He choked and felt his whole body go warm. "Uh, well, thanks for laying all that out so succinctly. I think those are two pretty compelling reasons why—"

"Not relevant."

"It seems pretty relevant to me," he said hotly.

She put down her notebook. Her old husky, Denali, snored softly in the corner. Retired from duty, he was a fixture in the office building. The colonel's face softened. "I love Katie like the family I never had. She wouldn't ask for help and that's why I'm determined to give it to her. Until her aunt returns to full strength, she needs us." She paused. "She needs *you*."

"But…"

"Remember when you first got Ella and she couldn't walk down the street without jumping in every puddle from here to Nome? We got advice from various experts that we should wash her out and start you with another dog."

He nodded.

"You didn't do that, did you? You doled out treats and positive praise and worked with her until she got through it. Remember?"

"Yes." He couldn't figure where the colonel was going with this.

"I want someone around Katie who's like that—determined, dedicated, averse to failure…"

He opened his mouth to remind her any of the squad would fit the bill.

"And gentle," she added. "With a touch of the goofball."

A touch of the goofball? For the life of him, Brayden did not know what to say. Should he feel flattered? Put upon? Worried about messing things up? "I…uh…"

Lorenza looked as though she'd set the universe right. "Details are that I hired two private security guards to patrol the ranch on a daily basis." She held up a hand. "The money comes from my own pocket, of course. The property is too remote and too big for you to handle round the clock, plus you have other duties. The security guys will wait to hear from you. Figured you'd want to plan their routes personally."

He hesitated. But what was he supposed to

do now? Pretend like his rocky past with Katie didn't matter?

"Did you want to say something, Trooper Ford?"

Did he? What excuse could he come up with to get out of this assignment? But the colonel was already looking at her paperwork again. "Addie will be in the hospital for a few days. She'll have protection there. If I know Katie, she'll be heading to the ranch as soon as possible. Do what's necessary to keep her safe."

He closed his mouth. "Yes, ma'am," he said, leaving the office and shutting the door behind him.

Ella sat on her haunches waiting for him in the hallway. Her eyebrows twitched as she regarded him, before a soft sigh ruffled her lips. "Do you think I'm a goofball, El?"

She swiped a wide pink tongue around her fleshy mouth and shook herself.

"You owe me, by the way," he said, bending to massage her neck. "The colonel doesn't know you still jump in puddles sometimes, and we're not even going to tell her about the case of the disappearing doughnuts from the staff room." Plans formed in his mind as he sauntered back with Ella through the office, heading for his SUV. *Check the security of the house, locks, windows, install motion detector lights.*

Design the most efficient routes for the security team... He was so lost in thought, he almost bumped into Helena and Poppy.

"What's up?"

"We went back today to the riverbank when the storm let up," Helena said. "We found something."

A tickle of dread flickered in his stomach. "What?"

"A dry suit, some empty cans and a waterproof sleeping bag in one of the caves Katie told us about," Poppy told him gravely. "Terrence has been staying there, using it as a base of operations, I would imagine, analyzing the ranch layout. He might return when things simmer down, to finish what he started."

To murder Addie and Katie.

And right then, he knew the colonel had been right in giving him the assignment, because every muscle in his body snapped to attention. Brayden would not let anything divert him. He was a trooper, first and foremost, and he would do his job, no matter who the protectee was. "He's not going anywhere but to jail. Come on, El. We've got to see a lady about a reindeer."

THREE

Katie's feet ached from pacing the hospital floors the night before. Now she was in her Anchorage apartment packing what she would need for her stay at the Family K, watering her plants and emptying the fridge of anything that would spoil.

These tasks did not quite keep her mind off the previous night's horror. Thinking about Aunt Addie lying lifeless on the dock made her go clammy all over. Brayden had sat awkwardly next to Katie at the hospital until the doctors assured her that the bullet had only penetrated the soft tissue of Addie's shoulder without impacting any major organs. Barring complications, her aunt was likely to recover fully, but it would be a long time before she was back to 100 percent.

He'd escorted Katie to her apartment, and she knew the local cops and some K-9 team members had driven by every hour or so to check that she was safely tucked away for the night.

Picturing Brayden and Ella circling her apartment made her feel simultaneously safe and skittish. He'd been so kind when she'd broken down, but her mortification rose every time she thought about snuggling up on his wide chest.

You know how he views you. And she wasn't anything like the tall, manicured, *reckless* woman he'd dated before. Looking back, she shouldn't have told him what she'd accidentally discovered about Jamie. But they were a family, Lorenza always said of her team, and what harmed one of them, harmed *all* of them. That "help" had backfired in a monumental way. She swallowed down a lump in her throat. Best not to think about it.

After pulling on a denim jacket and twisting her hair back into a clip, she waved at the local cop who had been parked outside her door since before dawn. At least it was not Brayden. The glorious morning made the horrifying incident with Terrence seem almost unreal, but the memory of it made her flesh crawl. Nothing was going to keep her from her aunt, even a murderous uncle.

Jaw set, she drove her Jeep to the hospital. All of her angst disappeared into a cloud of joy when the nurse told her Addie was awake and could have a visitor. Maybe she could allow herself to believe that Addie really was going to be all right. She nodded to the security guard stationed at her aunt's door.

Addie was pale and wan and looked so much older than she had the previous day. Deep lines grooved her forehead. An IV was attached to her arm and her wounded shoulder was heavily bandaged. She appeared to be sleeping.

"Good morning," Katie said softly.

Addie's eyes opened halfway. "Katie?"

She nodded.

Her aunt seemed relieved, the confusion clearing. "How are the babies?"

The *babies*...her reindeer. "They're fine. They were fed before... I mean...before Terrence showed up. The police drove by last night to check and everything was secure."

Addie shifted as if in pain. "I was stupid to go out to the dock, but it's always been my thinking place and I felt restless. I never dreamed I could be hurt on the Family K."

Katie hesitated for a few moments. "Can you tell me any more about Uncle Terrence?"

Addie flinched. "Don't call him that! He doesn't deserve to be your uncle."

Sensing her aunt had more to say, Katie stayed quiet.

"Terrence left home at eighteen, couldn't stand my parents' rules. He was always stubborn, hankering for an argument. I tried to find him when our parents passed. He didn't come for the funerals, though I posted notices in the paper thinking he'd see it. I did the same thing when your mother and father were killed." She scowled. "Why did I even try? After all, why would I expect him to care about our sister when he hadn't even shown his respect to our parents? *Stupid.* I never thought my brother, my own flesh and blood, would try to kill me." Addie paused. "And you. He would have murdered you, too."

Katie patted her arm. "Don't spend time thinking about that. You need to focus on healing."

Addie licked her dry lips, her gaze roving over Katie's face. "I wasn't a good aunt, was I? And I sure wasn't a great substitute mom, either."

Katie had never heard such talk from Addie. "You did your best. That's…"

Addie's jaw clenched. "Katie, I should have told you about Terrence, but I thought he'd vanished out of my life. I figured maybe he was dead. Good riddance since he was always a selfish, entitled jerk." She took a breath. "I saw his face there on the dock before he shot me, the way he spoke. He won't go away. He'll never quit. The best thing for you is to leave here, go somewhere safe where he won't find you." Her fingers squeezed Katie's arm so tight it hurt.

Katie kept her voice calm and controlled. "There would be no one to run the ranch if I left. I'll stay."

"I can't ask you to do that."

"You're not asking," Katie said.

Addie's face crumpled. Was it tears she saw in her aunt's eyes? Even at the funeral for Katie's parents Addie had not cried, just stood there as if she was carved from stone. "No. You have your own life to live. We'll have to find homes for the animals somehow. I'll sell the property when I can find a buyer." One crystal tear slid down her weathered cheek.

The Family K had been the hub of her aunt's world ever since Katie had known her. The only thing that made her smile was the reindeer. Katie had realized that, accepted it shortly after she'd come to live with Addie as a child. They'd tended the ranch together and that was how they connected. That single tear coursing down Addie's cheek washed away any misgivings in Katie's heart. In that moment she realized how much she loved her gruff, surly, single-minded aunt Addie. She'd never understood why God took her parents and her unborn brother in that crash, but she knew He'd not left her alone. Addie was right, she hadn't been much of a stand-in mom, but she'd done what she could, offered what she had, and Katie would do the same.

She cleared her throat. "Listen to me. You are not going to lose the ranch. I'm taking up the reins until you're better. It's my decision. I took time off from work. It's all arranged."

Addie pursed her lips as if she was struggling to keep from crying. "But…"

"It's settled," Katie insisted.

"Thank you," Addie breathed. Her aunt had never sounded so vulnerable before. "That means everything to me."

"You're welcome," she said, giving the other woman's hand a squeeze.

A shadow crossed over Addie's features. "But it's not safe. Terrence will find you, *hurt* you…"

"No, he won't."

Katie whirled to see Brayden standing in the doorway. Ella sat quietly at his side. "I'm not going to let your niece get hurt, ma'am. I've been assigned to make sure that doesn't happen."

Assigned? "But you've got other cases to work on," Katie protested. "What about—?"

"This one has risen to the top of the list," he said, cutting her off.

"So you'll look out for her?" Addie murmured, sagging in relief.

"Yes, ma'am. And we're going to arrest Terrence, too."

Katie looked at him, unsure what to say.

"I am glad you are feeling better, Ms. Kapowski. I'd smuggle you in some home-cooked food, but I've been told I am the worst cook in Alaska unless you want something grilled. That I can do." He turned his attention to her. "Katie, I'll be waiting in the hallway for you. Consider me your shadow." He did not smile as he turned away and marched out.

Her mouth went dry. "A shadow. Just what I need."

Addie's look went suddenly mischievous. "A very handsome shadow with a sense of humor. You two could…"

"No, we *couldn't*," Katie hurried to say, annoyed that she could feel a blush creeping up her neck. "We aren't compatible."

"How do you know until you try?"

Before Katie could set Addie straight, the woman launched into a set of directions. "The only way we're going to stay afloat is to hold that Christmas Fair. The planning meeting is on Friday. Everyone's already been invited. How can I leave that all up to you? I haven't even made the agenda yet."

"I won't tell you to relax, because I know you're not going to, so I'll just remind you that I'm very organized and I've been to the Christmas Fair every year since I was ten years old. I can do it, Aunt Addie. I'm sure the agenda hasn't changed much."

"But…" She winced in pain as she struggled to sit up higher.

"You've got a new phone since your other was damaged," Katie said firmly. "We'll have constant contact. I will call you if I need any clarification. You can text me if you think of anything that I might need to know. And you'll probably be home in a few days anyway, so you can take over the meeting."

A nurse came in. "I need to check vitals now, please."

Katie kissed the older woman's cheek. Addie gripped her arm, fingers rigid with intensity. "Be careful," her aunt whispered.

"I will." She forced a bright smile. "I've got a shadow, remember?" About that shadow… She'd be careful about the active threats, but extra vigilance would be necessary to keep her cool in front of Brayden Ford. She'd persevered in spite of him in the past and she would continue to do so now. Temporary partners. Settling on that descriptor put her on steady ground.

True to his word, Brayden drove behind

Katie from the hospital back to the Family K. She tried to ignore his presence as she ticked off the massive to-do list in her mind. The reindeer needed to be cared for and fed, the agenda for the Christmas Fair meeting would have to be generated, the house cleaned and snacks prepared. She'd need to recruit help since Addie's two ranch hands were gone. Hopefully with a little sweet-talking she could persuade a local to help her with all that. And she had just the person in mind.

Her thoughts strayed to the two missing animals... Aunt Addie's "babies." Thunder, the big male, and Lulu. Had Terrence stashed them somewhere to harass his sister? Killed the animals out of spite? The thought pained her as she pulled from Brighton Road onto the dirt access trail, temporarily bypassing the main house on her way to the pasture. Though she was hungry and her feet hurt, nothing could come before the care of the remaining reindeer.

She hurried to the pen, intending to examine them visually before opening the small holding area and freeing them into the vast pasture. Later, she would make sure they had an ample supply of alfalfa and willow leaves, but for the present, they were content to meander the sprawling property, nosing around. They were natural foragers, and their antlers enabled them to fork up lichen from under the Alaskan snows when winter blanketed the landscape. Until then, they'd eat leaves or grasses if available. There they were, outlined against a crystal-blue sky. What a sight. There was nothing more beautiful than a group of reindeer standing in pristine white snow, breathing puffs into the air.

Katie realized she considered the animals as her babies, too. The thought both pained and comforted her. Brayden and Ella joined her at the fence. Ella's nose twitched, but she did not seem excited to be so close to the reindeer. After all, there was no water at hand for her to splash in. "All present and accounted for?" Brayden said.

"Yes. Happy and healthy, as far as I can tell."

"What makes a reindeer happy?" he asked, helping to ease back the heavy gate.

The question surprised her. She pondered a moment. "They're like people, I guess. They need shelter, food and each other."

"Social."

"Very." She looked at the animals filing out.

"What's that clicking noise?"

"Their hooves," she explained. "They have an ankle tendon that rubs over the bone when they walk. It makes a clicking sound, which helps them find each other in snowy conditions. That's where the song comes from about the reindeer up on the house top…click, click, click."

"Wow. I did not know that. Handy to have your own tracking device. Keeping the family together, right?"

"Only a few of them are related, but they've become a family anyway." She chewed her lip, thinking about the missing members of the herd.

"We'll find them," Brayden said quietly, as if he'd read her mind.

Was she that transparent with her thoughts? "I hope so. If they were hurt, it would devastate my aunt."

"And you, too."

She felt his eyes on her and she ducked her chin. "Yes, me, too. I called a man from Palmer, on the way over. His name is Quinn and he's out of work right now, so he was happy to be offered a job."

"I know him. Good guy," Brayden said. "He's got two kids and one on the way, so that's a win for everyone. Plus, he's former army, so he knows how to handle himself. He'll be a good roomie 'cause he doesn't mind dogs."

"Roomie?"

Brayden nodded. "Sure. Ella and I are sacking out in the bunkhouse. I'm your shadow, remember?"

The bunkhouse? Brayden would actually be staying on the property 24/7? Well, of course he would. She resisted an eye roll. "Right." She swallowed. "I'll, uh, make sure it's ready for you both."

"Don't lift a finger. It's fine however it is. I backpacked through New Mexico one summer a few years ago, and believe me, I learned how to be grateful for any kind of shelter that doesn't involve sleeping on the ground, especially where there are fire ants. You ever sleep on a fire-ant nest? Talk about a rude awakening."

He was chatty. Nervously so? She got some sort of satisfaction out of knowing that he wasn't exactly indifferent to her presence. She noticed him glancing over the terrain, out toward the dock. He was looking for signs of Terrence. Swallowing hard, she refocused on the business. "I've got to get their immunizations done. And I'd better get started on the phone calls about the Christmas Fair planning meeting."

"Can I ask a favor first?"

He needed a favor? From *her*? "Of course."

"I missed breakfast, and not to be pushy, but

you did offer a peanut butter and jelly sandwich. I can fix it myself. Okay if I do that before you launch into the ranch agenda?" He added gently, "And I want to check over the main house real quick."

To make sure Uncle Terrence wasn't lying in wait?

A murderous uncle possibly lurking in the house and Brayden helping himself to the kitchen? She forced a light tone to match his. "Absolutely."

Brayden figured the isolation of the Family K was both a danger and an asset. The open terrain would make it easy to spot an approaching vehicle, yet the riverbank and the surrounding forest provided excellent concealment. It would be tricky to patrol all of it, but he'd instructed the private security people to report in, and he felt better knowing Quinn would be on the premises, as well.

"So what do you think, Ella?" he called into the back seat. He'd rolled the window down so she could get her share of interesting smells. She happily slobbered on the glass as she took in the surroundings. Best police protocol was to have a K-9 crated in the back seat, but at one hundred and fifteen pounds, Ella did not fit comfortably into any cage. She was a completely relaxed dog unless she was around the water or Brayden became upset for some reason. Her fine qualities made up for the occasional food-snatching incident. The term "gentle giant" really did capture Ella's essence.

As they drove to the main house, he analyzed Katie's reaction to his announcement that he was going to occupy the bunkhouse. She was surprised, yes, but clearly not pleased. No wonder. He remembered the feel of her in his arms, fragile and strong at the same time. Why did the memory refuse to leave his mind? On the heels of that recollection, another flooded in.

She needs us. She needs you, the colonel had said.

He was used to being needed on a professional level, wasn't he? This was no different. *You're on assignment, that's all.* But why him… with her? Yes, all the other officers were busy, but surely someone could have switched roles. His ego began to chatter. Was he being shuttled aside? Had he missed out on the bridal-party investigation for this smaller protection duty? Yet, somehow, it didn't feel in any way like a small thing to be safeguarding Katie Kapowski. And if he failed… The colonel would bring in someone else, which would be a blot on his career, yes, but failure meant that Katie would suffer. A nasty scene from his past scrolled through his mind.

A hesitant Katie. *"Jamie's using you."*

"What?"

"She was talking to some friends in the coffee shop. She said it was fun dating a good-looking cop, but that you were..." She cleared her throat. *"...too old and straitlaced for a long-term relationship."*

Shock and embarrassment had flooded through him, quickly concealed behind anger. *"You must have misunderstood."*

"No, I didn't. I'm sorry."

"Sorry? I don't think so. You're telling me this, why? To get back at me for your interview?"

She'd flushed, turned on her heel, and that was it.

Things had gone from bad to worse after that with Jamie and he eventually realized Katie was telling him the truth, but he still figured he'd been right about her motive in revealing it to him. He'd hurt her, she believed, and she'd retaliated. The score was even. But it sure didn't feel like they were competing anymore, did it? Frankly, he wasn't sure what he felt except the strong desire to get the job done and leave the ranch as soon as possible.

They passed the small storage sheds and he

added that to his tasks for the day. They would all need to be checked and secured. Mulling over the tactical aspects of the ranch security put him back on professional footing. Trooper stuff... That he could do. His boss was counting on him.

Katie hauled a small bag out of her car and headed for the front door while he freed Ella from the back seat. Brayden noted that the old building was clearly in need of some TLC. The cedar siding was warped in some places, and staining on the steep roof indicated some leakage might have occurred. Such was the nature of buildings in Alaska. Harsh weather contributed to never-ending repair needs. He doubted the ranch brought in much of a profit. It was truly a labor of love for Addie and now for Katie.

And there he was, staring at her again. Her hair shone almost coppery in the morning sunlight, her stride determined as she approached the front door. He was mentally admonishing himself for daydreaming when it hit him. *The door.* The old levered handle was turned down just slightly, as if the locking mechanism hadn't completely caught. Something was preventing it from shutting properly.

He bolted forward, shouting, "Katie, don't!" Ella barked at Brayden's frantic tone.

With her fingers still on the handle, Katie half turned. He grabbed her wrist and pulled her backward. As he did so, the door swung open. There was a tremendous crash. Something fell, scattering debris everywhere.

"Stay here with Ella," he commanded. Katie's eyes were wide as Brayden pushed through the door. The closed drapes left it gloomy, but there was enough light to make out the booby trap. A can of nails wedged above the door, waiting to fall when it was pushed open. It was heavy enough that it might have fractured her skull if he hadn't pulled her back in time.

He stood there, vision adjusting to the dim light, half crouched, listening.

Only one question remained.

Was Katie's murderous uncle hiding somewhere in the house, waiting to see if his booby trap worked? Gripping his revolver, Brayden eased step by step into the house.

Terrence wasn't going to vanish this time.

That was a promise.

FOUR

Ella pressed close to Katie's side. They waited together, Katie's heart slamming against her ribs. She was alternately terrified and furious. This was her aunt's home, the only place where she'd felt secure after her parents died. The ranch was the sanctuary where Addie had helped her put the pieces of herself back together, and now it had been violated.

Good old Uncle Terrence? Had to be. Thinking about him possibly lying in wait for Brayden made her body ice over. Ella was agitated as well, whining slightly, gaze riveted on the open door. Minutes passed. Should she call for backup? Her thoughts branched in all directions, like lightning forking the tundra.

Footsteps made them both go tense. If it was Terrence, what would she do? Scream and run? Throw rocks or whatever else she could find at him? Stomach flipping, she waited. Brayden appeared in the doorway, holstering his weapon and carefully stepping around the debris. "Nobody inside."

She let out a breath she hadn't known she was holding. Gone, and still at large.

Brayden beckoned her. "Come inside through the garage. I've got Gabriel coming to help check for prints and photograph, and the security guard is driving the perimeter, but I don't think we'll find much. Terrence obviously set this all up and took off. If anything, he's watching from a distance."

All those trees on the neighboring property. She shivered.

Dutifully, Ella and Katie circled around to the garage so the booby-trap evidence could be photographed and prints taken. She noticed how Brayden waited until she was settled in a kitchen chair.

His brow furrowed as he clicked off his phone. In a few moments a man in a security outfit joined them. He was almost as tall as Brayden, but rail thin with a shining bald head.

"I'm Phil," he said, shaking Katie's hand. "Alex is my counterpart. I'm sorry about what happened. No sign of anyone on the main roads. Maybe he crawled up from the riverbank again?"

Brayden scowled. "I'll get a team on that.

When Alex gets here for his shift, I'll fill him in. I'm going to install a camera on the house, but for now, let's increase the patrols around the riverbank and the forested area next to the north and south pens."

"Yes, sir," Phil said. "I'll start on that right now."

When the security officer left, Brayden started to prowl the kitchen. "I'll make you tea," he said.

"Thank you, but I'm okay, really."

Her words didn't seem to make a dent. "Tea is what people drink in times of crises, I'm pretty sure. I don't care for the stuff myself, but I recall after my parents split my mother must have felt cups of tea would make it all okay since she fixed it every time my sisters and I stayed with her. My folks had joint custody." He rooted around in the cupboard, knocking over a box of pancake mix.

He appeared filled with intense energy. Her hands were shaking, and her pulse was still rocketing. Patrols of the property? Hiding places along the riverbank? A forest full of places for Terrence to conceal himself?

It was almost too crazy to believe.

He was on to the next cupboard. "Where do you keep the tea bags?"

"Brayden?"

His voice was muffled by the cupboard. "Am I getting warm?"

"Brayden," she said again, a bit louder this time.

Now he looked at her. She pointed to a carousel in the corner that held individual pods. "We're coffee drinkers, not tea. And we have a machine, but I appreciate you working so hard at it."

He quirked a smile. "Ah. Well, then. Care for a cup of coffee?"

"If you'll have one." Had she sounded coy? She desperately hoped not. Talking to Brayden was chore enough. She'd never think about flirting. She was trying to conjure a follow-up comment when he sighed.

"I have never passed up a cup of coffee yet." He poured in water and busied himself with the procedure until he produced two steaming mugfuls.

"Gabriel's nearby, so he'll be here in a few." Brayden added two spoonfuls of sugar and a packet of dried creamer to his drink. She wondered how he kept such a narrow waist if he doctored his coffee on a regular basis.

Katie let the warmth of the mug seep into her palms. She cleared her throat and said, "If you hadn't noticed the door was not shut properly, I'd be next to Aunt Addie in the hospital with a fractured skull or worse." A polite thank-you was all she'd meant, but the words made her eyes brim. "Why does Terrence hate me so much? We'd never even met before he held me at gunpoint."

"Because he doesn't know you. If he did, I can't see how he wouldn't like you."

His eyes were a mesmerizing iridescent green, and she found herself caught by the color and his sentiment. Brayden was being kind. That was all.

"You hated me," she said softly. "For telling you about Jamie."

His cheeks went red and he sank down at the table. "*Hate* is a strong word." His eyes found hers. "Why did you tell me about her, anyway? The truth."

Now it was her turn to shift in the chair. "I wasn't going to, but something changed my mind."

"What?"

Katie shrugged, withdrawing into her shell. "Not important."

He paused, perhaps to see if she would answer after all. "Anyway, you were right…about Jamie. I didn't believe you, but it wasn't long before it all came out. I was an idiot not to suspect. She wanted to talk about my job all the time, but not much of anything else. And she made excuses to bring her friends by to see me when I was on duty, but I lost my allure when I was dressed in civvies. Plus, she got a good laugh out of my choice of movies and music and such. I guess I was probably the source of a lot of humor for her and her friends."

"I'm sorry."

His face grew pained. "Too bad we couldn't have ended things amicably, but that was out the window when I arrested her. She didn't take it well."

Katie tried to look surprised, but the gossip had spread like lightning throughout the force. She kept quiet and let him say it.

"She was driving under the influence with a car full of her young friends."

Young friends. One of the reasons he'd advised against hiring Katie. Too young and inexperienced. That opinion probably hadn't changed. The conversation was becoming *way* too personal. "Thank you for the coffee." She sipped from her mug. "Maybe your mom was on to something. Could be it doesn't matter that it's coffee or tea. Drinking something warm is medicinal."

"Mom always tried to fix everything. The divorce was the one thing she couldn't fix."

"How old were you?" she asked.

"Twelve."

"That's a hard age to have your family split up."

He sighed. "They both loved me, I know that, but I always got the feeling when I was pin-balled between them that Dad took me out of duty, not the desire to spend time with me. Not ideal. Made me realize that a broken marriage is worse than no marriage at all." A muscle ticked in his jaw. "Maybe that's why lately I don't seek out relationships, that and the Jamie fiasco."

"We all have our reasons."

He arched a brow. "You, too? I wondered why you and John didn't stick."

Of course he knew about her brief relationship with local attorney John Fitzgerald. Now her face was positively crimson, she was sure. "He is a good man, but we wanted different things."

"Like what?" He grimaced. "Wait. Nosy, right?"

"He's on the fast track to marriage."

"And you don't want that?" he murmured.

"Not right now."

"What *do* you want, Katie?"

She looked him in the eye when she answered. "I want to be good at my job, to prove that I can stand on my own."

"Not one for letting others hold your hand. I noticed that. To be honest, I thought it was standoffishness at first. But I get it now. You're independent."

The words floated out before she could bite them back. "I'm afraid not to be." *Afraid?* What was she doing blabbering on to Brayden Ford about her fears?

"Because your family died when you were a child?" His voice was soft.

How had he put his finger squarely on it? "Everyone I relied on was gone in a minute. Aunt Addie took me in and taught me to take care of myself."

"Does that mean someone else can't take care of you, too?"

How had she gotten into this conversation? Too much. She'd shared too much. Now all she could do was offer a tight smile. "Doesn't seem like we should go too deeply into my psyche right now."

"Of course, right. Sorry to pry." He fiddled with his mug and spilled some liquid on the table. Mopping it up with a paper towel, he shot a look of chagrin at her. "I am beginning to understand why the colonel thinks I am a goofball."

Katie laughed. "It's a term of endearment, probably. She knows you are a great trooper."

He cocked his head. "I'm not so sure. Figured if she did, she'd want me on the Violet James case..." He broke off abruptly.

"Instead of babysitting me?"

His cheeks went dusky. "No. I didn't mean that."

She pulled her eyes away. He had meant it and now she understood. Lorenza had assigned him to her case when he would much prefer being in on the manhunt for the two men who had committed murder and framed Violet James for it. Why wouldn't he? The entire team had been on fire to close the case, especially Hunter McCord, who'd promised to rescue his fiancée's best friend. "More incentive for you to catch my uncle, right? Close the case and get back to the manhunt."

"That came out wrong. Big surprise. I'm glad to be here at the Family K. Really, Katie." He placed a hand over hers. Her brain demanded that she pull away immediately, but her heart relished the feel of his strong fingers on hers. "I don't look at this as babysitting. You are... I mean, I've had great respect for you since you came aboard."

In spite of his reluctance. At least he *had* come to value her work. His touch was warm and encouraging. Talking with Brayden was like tending an untamed reindeer. Sometimes smooth and easy, but most of the time tense and strained. "It's okay," she said, finding the strength to pull away. "You don't have to explain anything. Hopefully, you'll arrest Terrence soon and this mess will all be over."

Then Brayden could return to his heart's desire, catching the murderer who was waiting to ambush Violet.

Brayden started to speak again when Gabriel Runyon entered through the garage door with a camera and his Saint Bernard, Bear, by his side. Gabriel was a tall man, as tall as Brayden, but Bear stood nearly to his waist. The K-9 greeted Ella with a tail wag as Gabriel joined them.

"Hey, Katie. We miss you at the office. No one knows where anything is, and we forgot everything we ever learned about the Wi-Fi. That and the colonel is irritable without you."

"I miss you all, too." *And my job. Especially now that things are getting so awkward with a reluctant babysitter around.* Maybe she had made a mistake taking on the Family K, but how could she turn her back on it?

Gabriel listened to the details of the most recent incident from Brayden.

"He's getting pretty brazen, isn't he?" The two men exchanged a knowing look. She didn't need to have a badge to decipher it. Terrence was becoming a loose cannon, heedless of the risk of capture. Armed and very dangerous, their look said.

"All right. I'll photograph the scene," Gabriel said. "Figured out the point of entry?"

"Window jimmied in the back. I'm going to get some alarms installed today."

Gabriel readied his camera.

"What's the word on the James case?" Brayden asked.

"Helena figures she's been coming to Anchorage to visit a clinic, but we are still checking. The docs are pretty close-lipped about their patients, and she undoubtedly used a fake name, so it's slow going." Gabriel blew out a breath. "Where has she been holing up the rest of the time? That's the big question. And how can a very pregnant woman be so hard to find?"

Katie tried not to listen in, but she'd been part of the whole investigation since April, when the murder of tour guide Cal Brooks occurred and Violet had been framed for it. That was the main case Brayden should be working on—a pregnant woman at risk of being killed, vulnerable and alone.

Vulnerable and alone. Those words struck a chord in her own heart. She fought back against them, willing away the feeling of helplessness she'd felt in the back seat of her parents' wrecked car so long ago, silent except for the sound of her own crying and the drip of gasoline on the snow.

You're not alone, Katie reminded herself. She had the security guards and Aunt Addie coming home soon, and Quinn would arrive to start work any moment now. Let Brayden install his cameras and whatever else he decided they needed to keep Terrence away, and then she'd prove to him she didn't need a babysitter.

He could go back to his life and she to hers. Case closed.

Brayden got a broom and helped Katie sweep up the nails after Gabriel left. He detected a coolness in her, probably after he'd stuck his foot in his mouth earlier. There was truth in his dumb remark—he did miss being out of the loop on the James case—but he did not see his current detail as babysitting. As a matter of fact, he discovered the more time he spent around Katie, the more he enjoyed it. There was something about her, something genuine and intelligent and strong. Her life had imploded at age ten, his at twelve. Though she didn't want to share much with him, he understood they had more in common than he'd realized.

That line of thinking was unprofessional and unsafe, he scolded himself. When Katie left him in search of Addie's address book, he breathed easier. Now he could focus on installing the window alarms and cameras he'd asked Phil to bring. Then once that was done, he would have to mentally prepare himself for the next big challenge...the Christmas Fair planning event the next day. He'd tried to talk her into postponing, but that hadn't gone well. And he honestly didn't blame her. The ranch was on the brink of going under. That much was clear. Katie was working on getting him a list of the attendees and their car license numbers and models, which he would pass on to Phil and Alex.

Ella turned her massive head as a motorcycle approached.

Quinn, the local man Katie had hired, got off, jammed his helmet on his handlebar and limped over. Brayden got down off the stepladder and shook his hand.

"Nice to see you again," Brayden said. "You okay? That knee looks painful."

Quinn grimaced and scrubbed a hand over his fuzzy beard. "Wish I had a better story to tell. Tripped on the sidewalk and landed on the knee I already injured in the service. I can't work as a painter until I can do ladders again." He lowered his voice. "I...didn't want to tell the boss in case she'd think I can't do the work."

"Too late," Katie said from the doorway. "Cat's out of the bag."

Quinn looked at his feet. "Aw, sorry about that, Miss Kapowski. I should have been upfront about the knee, but I really need the job. Rent's due at the end of the month."

"You can call me Katie, and it's okay. I know you'll be all right with the reindeer. They don't need much wrestling anyway, except during hoof trimming, and that's been done recently."

Relief spread across his features. "I appreciate it, more than you know. Wife and kids are visiting Grandma for a couple of weeks, so I can stay the nights, easy. I'll do whatever you need done without complaint. I really appreciate the work."

"And I appreciate your help, too," Katie said. "Go ahead and get settled in the bunkhouse, and we can talk after. There's no kitchen, but I can cook well enough to keep you all alive. Sorry, I don't cook meat, though."

Quinn laughed. "I'll lay in a supply of beef jerky."

"You'll have to keep it safe from a meat-eating machine," Brayden advised, pointing to Ella. "I've seen this stalwart officer of the law swipe a kid's hot dog without the slightest show of remorse."

"Yes, sir. I'll keep a sharp lookout," Quinn said.

"Okay. Let me know if either of you needs anything." Katie headed back to the main house.

Brayden watched until she made it inside, locked the door and waved. It was quite an inconvenience to keep the door locked, he was sure, but she'd uttered no complaint. He walked Quinn to the wood-sided bunkhouse. "I might as well see it, too, since we're roomies."

The inside was a simple cabin setup. Two small bedrooms, each with a single bed, and one bathroom no bigger than a closet. The bedrooms had windows, but in the primary living area Brayden was sorry to find there were no windows that looked directly out on the main house, only a small one set up high in the wall to improve lighting. The bunkhouse was built for functionality, not aesthetics.

Ella padded to one of the open bedroom doors, waddled on in and heaved herself up on the bed. Brayden and Quinn watched in surprise.

Quinn chuckled. "Uh… So I'm guessing that's gonna be your room."

"Looks that way. I'll bring her cushion in from the car and try to explain to her once again that she's a dog."

Quinn tossed his duffel on the other bed.

"Good enough for me. With three kids, I'll take any kind of quiet I can get."

"Well, this kind of quiet is likely going to be broken by dog snoring."

"Better than kid noise, trust me." He hesitated. "Been hearing things in town. About Terrence."

"I'll fill you in on the ways he's been terrorizing the ranch. But what have you heard?"

"That he shot Addie and maybe stole those reindeer that went missing. Fact or gossip?"

"Fact on the shooting. Only theory on the reindeer for now, but pretty likely." Brayden told him about the booby trap.

"Can't think of a reason anyone would do that kind of thing, except for one." Quinn's mouth tightened. "Hatred, pure and simple."

Brayden exhaled. "Yeah. That's why I'm here along with two security guards and now you. Consider yourself deputized to help in any way if Katie's safety is in danger, but don't put yourself at risk."

"Think he's given up?"

Brayden didn't hesitate. "Nope."

They dropped their bags in their respective rooms and looked at diagrams of the ranch property. Brayden pointed out the places he felt were most vulnerable. "No way to secure the entire riverbank, and the dock is out of camera range of the main house. Wi-Fi here is terrible."

They studied and discussed until Katie rejoined them, frowning. "I found the list of attendees for tomorrow. You're not going to like it."

He arched an eyebrow. "Let's have it. How many?"

"Fourteen." She stopped his reply with an outstretched palm. "I know you think we should cancel."

"Not cancel, *postpone*. Until Terrence is in custody."

"There is no telling how long that will take. We can't delay the planning meeting any longer or we run into conflicts with Thanksgiving and Christmas. We're already down to the wire. It's now or never." He saw her anguish, though she kept her expression sedate.

"Maybe there's another way," Brayden said. "We can brainstorm."

"If there was a way to keep this ranch afloat without the fair, don't you think we would have tried it?" Her eyes flashed fire.

He should have figured she'd blow through any pie-in-the-sky "it's gonna be all right" sentiments. She might have made a fine cop, he thought, admiringly.

"We are completely dependent on donations

and we never know how many mouths we'll need to feed," she said. "Last spring we rescued two babies whose mother died of disease and a full-grown male from a foreclosed ranch and he had to have surgery for an ulcer. The bills never stop. Neither can the Christmas Fair."

Her chin was tipped upward, mouth set into a firm line. He wondered at that moment what it would be like to kiss those determined lips. *Whoa, fella. Let's try to keep some sort of control on your ridiculous imagination.* The experience with Jamie should have taught him that. "Understood," he said, shooing the thought away. "What's the itinerary?"

"We'll meet in the house at ten tomorrow morning. After the meeting, Addie usually shows everyone the animals and gives a family history of the herd so the volunteers can share with visitors when the time comes. We provide bag lunches and people sit at the picnic tables outside to plan their individual parts of the fair."

"Such as…?"

She ticked off the items on her fingers. "The barbecue area, sleigh rides, reindeer meet and greet, snowshoeing lessons, pictures with a reindeer…"

"Man. This sounds like the best event in town. All right. Fourteen people it is. We'll keep the house secure and I'll see if I can recruit some help to monitor the tour and picnic."

"Great," she said.

"And you," he said with a smile, "will have the undivided attention of a large black dog and one clumsy state trooper."

Her cheeks took on a fetching shade of pink and she looked away.

Quinn shifted. "Would Terrence actually target the visitors?"

"I would have said no a few days ago, but booby-trapping the house and shooting Addie are pretty brazen. His primary target is…"

"Me," Katie said.

Her expression was calm and courageous, but he didn't miss the quick ripple of fear that passed across her face.

He won't get near you, Brayden promised silently. "If he shows, we'll arrest him. Since I can't talk you out of postponing…"

"I won't do anything risky," Katie said, "but I have to make sure this ranch succeeds and we find the missing animals." Her voice hitched. "Lulu came to us pregnant. She had her baby in June, so he's four months old now. His name is Sweetie. He's not thriving since his mother's been taken. They normally nurse for six months, so we've been supplementing with bottles, but it's not optimal and he's underweight.

I don't want to think about him going into the winter months without his mother. We just have to get her back soon."

He saw from the way Quinn did not meet Katie's eye that he did not believe the animals were still alive. And despite his own fears, Brayden truly wished he could share Katie's hopefulness about a good outcome. For her sake *and* the animals that she and Addie loved so dearly. Those reindeer were a tight family and that was a rare thing in this world. He knew that much from painful experience. Katie wasn't in a hurry to marry into a human family, but she was sure enough tight with her antlered one.

"All right. Cameras are up. Next order of the day is to search the storage units and secure them. You and I will have the keys, Quinn, no one else."

"Roger that," the other man said. "I might as well go with you now and see where everything is that I'm going to need."

Katie walked off the porch first. Avoiding him or focused on her to-do list?

He paused a moment to take in the sweep of vast acreage, the solitude broken by the wind and the tumbling waves of the nearby Frontier River. He wasn't deluding himself. All the security measures he could put into place were only inconveniences to a resourceful relative who knew the ranch.

A man fueled by hatred.

And hatred was a powerful force indeed.

FIVE

Katie toyed with her necklace, groaning as she perused the shopping list dictated by her aunt Addie early that morning. "Fourteen people can eat a lot."

"Especially carnivores," Brayden said mischievously. They'd decided to take her Jeep to the grocery store in town since his car was filled with too much equipment and dog gear to fit the necessary supplies.

She couldn't help it. Babysitter or not, she was glad for his company. Sometimes it seemed as if there was no awkwardness or age gap between them and that they were meeting for the first time instead of sharing an uncomfortable past.

They drove along the main street. Most of the storefronts hadn't changed much over the years. "I used to come here with Aunt Addie for the Friday Fling Farmers' Market." She recalled the white tents that would line the street in the summer months. "My favorite was the honey. Sweetest I ever tasted. Addie isn't a great cook, so I learned how to make biscuits for us. That was sort of our treat, homemade biscuits with Friday Fling honey." She bit her lip.

"Thinking about Addie?"

She nodded. "She's gruff and ornery, but deep down she is made of gold."

Brayden's look was sympathetic. "She'll be all right. Home before you know it. Doctors are optimistic about her recovery, right?"

"Yes. She's stubborn, though, and I don't see her convalescing like she'd supposed to at the Family K. I'm more concerned with having her come home when Terrence is still bent on destroying the ranch."

He squeezed her lower forearm. The gesture surprised her and somehow felt natural at the same time. Confusing.

"One good thing about his recklessness. He's going to slip up. They always do. We'll get him. You can take that to the bank."

Her cheeks went warm at his earnest tone. Almost as if he cared personally. No, it was just the job. He said he shied away from relationships as much as she did, probably more so after Jamie. What a shame, she thought. Brayden Ford would be a wonderful spouse for someone. Maybe down the road he'd find his soul mate. She wondered why the thought gave her a pang.

She noted he checked the rearview mirror from time to time. He was also carrying his weapon and a badge clipped to his waist, though he wore jeans and a soft T-shirt that brought out the jade in his eyes. He was not off duty on this errand, probably never would be around her.

Jamie had been fortunate to have a man like Brayden courting her, even if she couldn't see that.

She got out and he took up position at her elbow. Ella lumbered along, too, nose quivering. The dog's state trooper vest was a free pass to go anywhere with Brayden, but she knew he'd need to keep an eagle eye on his canine around the food items. She enjoyed the feel of Brayden's strong arm against her shoulder, the clean, spicy fragrance of his soap.

He ushered her into the store, and they walked to the deli counter. Brayden struck up a friendly chat with the butcher before he turned to Katie.

Charlie the butcher measured out the meats and wrapped them. His lips pursed under his full mustache. "I heard about what happened to Addie."

Katie's smile dimmed. "Yes. Thankfully my prayers were answered and she's going to be okay."

"She's a tough customer. Knows what she wants and gets it."

Was that criticism? Katie knew her aunt's faults, but she wasn't about to let some stranger add his two cents. She stiffened. "I love my aunt. She's been great to me."

"No offense meant." He chuckled. "Don't get me wrong. I like her a lot. Have for ages. As a matter of fact, I'm on the fair planning committee this year."

"Oh, of course. I recognize your name now from the planning meeting list."

He nodded. "I've been trying to get her to let me take her out to dinner. She's my kind of person—no-nonsense, takes care of her business and doesn't ask for handouts. Love a strong woman like Addie. That's why I was planning to call and tell you."

"Tell us what?" Brayden said.

He scanned the empty aisle and leaned forward, voice low. "I think I saw him."

"Who?"

"Terrence."

She could feel the tension emanating off Brayden like electrical waves as he responded. "When and where?"

"Yesterday. Cops came around a few weeks ago and showed us pictures of him, and I'm almost positive the same guy came into our store. I told the owner that it was him shopping real early in the morning, right after we opened, but he says I'm seeing things. The guy was bearded, wearing glasses, but you can fake those things, huh?"

Terrence had been in this store? Goose bumps erupted along her arms.

Brayden was listening attentively. "What made you think it was him?"

"The demeanor mostly, I guess. Everyone is friendly around here, good at small talk, except for Addie, maybe." He grinned. "Anyhow, this guy didn't want to shoot the breeze. Came in, got what he wanted, headed for the checkout."

"Do you have an in-store camera?" Brayden asked.

"Uh-huh. Cheapie one, super old, but it works. I'll get the key and tell the manager."

Katie felt dazed as she followed Brayden and Charlie to a cramped workroom where Charlie shoved an old-fashioned videotape into the slot. The picture came to life, grainy and gray as a time clock ticked away at the bottom right corner. At 6:35 a.m., a man walked into view. He was indeed bearded, with glasses, and he seemed to hunch over as he disappeared down an aisle. When he came into view again carrying a hand basket, Brayden stopped the video and took pictures with his phone.

"What do you think, Katie? You're the only one who's seen him close-up except for your aunt. Is it Terrence?"

She continued to watch the tape as it started up again. The man was careful to keep his face down, paying with a ten-dollar bill fished from his pocket. He gathered his bag and strolled away from the counter, but she'd seen enough. The profile, chin tucked to his chest, prominent ears, grizzled brows.

"That's him," she whispered.

"Did you see what vehicle he drove? Which direction he took when he left?"

"I'm sorry." Charlie sighed. "I had a shipment coming in, so I had to get back to the deli counter. That's why I haven't had a moment to call you, either."

Brayden rewound the tape and they watched it again. She was not sure what he was looking for until he froze on the spot where the man put his basket on the counter for the cashier to scan.

Bread.

Peanut butter.

Carrots.

And one more item that made the breath congeal in her lungs.

Several rolls of duct tape.

Outside, Brayden hurried to open the passenger door for Katie, but Ella had stopped dead in front of him and he almost took a header over her. Her nose quivered as she sampled the air. Suddenly she started to bark, her hoarse vocalizations deafening.

"Katie, go back in the…" he started.

But a car suddenly careened into view, driving right up onto the sidewalk. Terrence was behind the wheel. In a matter of moments, he would plow right into them. Brayden drew his gun and fired into the windshield, but the car didn't slow. It grazed a newspaper machine, which was knocked from its bolts and launched right at him. He spun to the side and fell, rolling several times before he smacked into the brick facade of the store.

Charlie came out at a gallop. "What's going on?"

Brayden was scrambling to his feet. Terrence's car was empty now, front end smashed from the impact with the newspaper machine, engine still revving… And Katie was gone. "Call the local police," he yelled at Charlie.

Ella sprinted to the fenced alley between the

shop and the building next to it, barking for all she was worth. She had to be following Katie. He took off in pursuit. Ella's barking echoed and bounced along the narrow walls. As he, too, rounded the corner, he saw the dog chasing after Terrence, Katie a few steps ahead of him. She turned to look back, eyes huge with fear. As she did so, she stumbled and went down.

Ella barked, skidding to an ungainly stop as Terrence closed in on Katie. The dog was confused, unsure what to do.

"Stop! Alaska state trooper!" Brayden yelled. He didn't have a clean shot. Ella was in between them and Katie just behind Terrence. There was no way he could risk a bullet hitting either one of them.

Ella broke off from barking at Terrence and decided to make a run for Katie. As the mountain of a dog raced toward him, Terrence leaped up, grabbed the top of the fence and heaved himself over. Brayden holstered his weapon and did the same. He clawed his way up and dropped on the other side, yanking out his gun again.

A startled maintenance worker stood immobilized, holding a trash bag. He stabbed a forefinger at the alley, which exited onto the street. "Guy ran that way."

Brayden started in again, sprinting for all he was worth. Arriving at the street, panting, he looked both ways, just in time to see Terrence hopping into a departing bus. He yelled and tried to wave down the driver, but the vehicle was already pulling away. Frustration burning like wildfire through him, he phoned in to the local cops to shadow the bus route. But Terrence wouldn't be on it, he thought with a sinking heart. As soon as he was out of sight, he'd pull the stop cord and demand to get off.

He ran back to find Katie limping from the alley, Ella glued to her side. As fast as possible, he urged her back to the safety of the Jeep, which had escaped damage. Inside, he called the colonel as they sped away from town. Then, as they drove, he briefed the local PD about the sequence of events that had just transpired.

His pulse was still thudding intensely five minutes later. The wide streets were quiet save for the occasional car. Couples on errands, ranchers who offered friendly waves as they rolled along. He was still on the lookout, expecting to see Terrence at any moment, and he knew Katie was, too, but there was no sign of him. He'd vanished, like smoke.

Brayden shot a look in the rearview at Ella. "You know, for an underwater search-and-rescue dog, you really saved the day. Extra treats for you, big girl."

Katie still said nothing.

He wanted to take her hand, but she was rigid with tension. "Your knee okay?"

"Just scraped."

"We'll get him," he said.

"Do you really believe that?"

Brayden knew she was too smart for false reassurances, but still he offered her a smile. "It's a matter of time before we bring him down. That's the honest truth. Don't worry." He almost rolled his eyes at his own platitude. *Don't worry* had to be the most useless phrase in the English language. When had that sage advice ever made someone stop fretting? The woman had almost been flattened moments ago or abducted. Terrible possibilities rolled through his mind.

She seemed to read his mind. "So it's nothing to worry about that Terrence was in the store buying duct tape?"

Katie was sharp. He should have known she wouldn't have missed that detail. He cleared his throat. "The bigger problem for me is how he knew we were going to be shopping just then."

"He's got a source? Some helpful shopkeeper whom he's paying?" Katie shrugged, a casual gesture that did not ease the tension in the line of her shoulders. "If Terrence wants my aunt to give him the ranch, maybe he's decided to kidnap me to force her to comply. He might have hoped he'd knock me out with the bucket of nails and come back to get me. When that didn't work, he decided to snatch me outside the store."

"I'm not sure he's thinking that clearly. His acts have been reckless, thus far."

The morning sunshine caught her hair and set it aglow. He wanted to reach out and comb his fingers through it. To soothe her after everything she'd just been through…

"Or maybe he wants to punish my aunt by taking me away from her."

He tugged gently at a copper strand. It was soft satin, as he'd imagined. "Hey there. We're going to keep you safe, Ella and I. Don't let your fears carry you away." His teasing gesture did not produce any effect. "Tell me what else."

She stared out the windshield. "I was worrying that there might be another motive brewing in Terrence's mind. He probably knows that I am next in line to own the ranch, since my aunt has no children. Maybe he wants to try to force me to change the will after he kills Addie."

He took her hand. Though his tone was Mr. Cool, his gut was vibrating like a plucked wire. What if Ella hadn't been there to bark a warning as Terrence careened toward Katie? "Let's not get ahead of ourselves. We have no hard evidence about what Terrence is planning, only supposition."

When she didn't pull away from his grasp, he allowed himself to savor the closeness. Her skin was warm, like the woman herself.

I'll take care of you, his heart whispered. The startling thought caused him to let go. She was his boss's assistant, he reminded himself. Much *younger* assistant. He'd wanted to take care of Jamie, too, and instead he'd turned out looking about as dim as Alaska in December. Katie had no doubt enjoyed telling him about his girlfriend's betrayal, though she didn't admit it.

"The carrots," Katie said, pulling him from his self-recrimination.

"What?"

"The carrots Terrence was buying at the store. Addie said Terrence never showed any interest in the reindeer, so he wouldn't know."

"Know what?"

"It's a misconception that reindeer eat carrots, probably due to the whole Santa business. The truth is, reindeer have no front incisors on the top, so it's hard for them to eat, much less digest, carrots. We don't feed them to our reindeer. When we allow guests to offer food, it's willow leaves or lichen."

"What do the carrots in Terrence's basket tell you?"

She began to twist her necklace around one

finger. "That he's bought into the misconception. He was buying that big bunch of carrots to feed the reindeer he stole."

"Could be he was just buying them to eat himself."

She eyed him. "Would you? A bachelor who is buying bread and peanut butter, would you really buy a bulk bag of carrots that you'd have to peel yourself to eat or cook?"

"No."

"That was Terrence," she said. "I know it. And he has our reindeer. They have to be close. Where could he be keeping them?"

"I'll alert the team and have them search."

Her brows were drawn into a V. "The reindeer won't stay healthy. He doesn't know how to care for them."

Brayden saw she was starting to breathe fast. He took her hand again. "They are strong animals. Big, too. He can't keep them hidden for long."

She blinked. "He's done a pretty good job of it so far."

He considered his next comment. It probably wasn't appropriate for him to share his spiritual thoughts in the present circumstance. When he'd tried with Jamie, she'd started calling him Preacher. Katie was his job, his duty, and they were professional colleagues, nothing more, but he felt compelled to share anyway. "You know what my mom used to say? God is for us, even when we're losing, so keep your eyes up, not down."

Katie's glance was puzzled. "Like Romans?"

He grinned. "Yes. You know your Bible. She was speaking about Romans 8:31. I've seen a lot of things, *bad* things, during my time in law enforcement. When I was a rookie, it would eat me up sometimes. I'd ask my mom, so if God is for us, why are things so bleak in this world? She said, God walks us through the struggles, and He's promised us the win. Eyes up, not down."

To his surprise, he saw tears well in Katie's eyes. She detached herself from him to pull a tissue from her pocket.

Foot in mouth again, Ford? "I'm sorry," he said. "I didn't mean to make you cry."

"They are happy tears, believe it or not."

He'd never really understood the concept of happy tears, but he was glad he hadn't added to her sadness. Ella shoved her head in from the back seat and licked the side of Katie's neck, which set her to giggling. When her giggles subsided, she continued.

"After my parents died in the wreck, I was crippled by fear. Living out in the middle of nowhere on a ranch didn't help, I guess. I wouldn't sleep with the lights off and I didn't want to go to school. Aunt Addie finally walked into my bedroom late one night and opened the Bible. She took a highlighter and underlined Romans 8:31. She said in her typical grumpy way, 'Katie, are you gonna believe Him or not? He's smarter than you and He promised. All you gotta do is believe Him.'" She laughed. "There were not warm, fuzzy pep talks from Aunt Addie."

"She's a to-the-point lady," Brayden said.

"True. Funny thing is, I made my choice and somehow God got me out of bed every day and back into life. It wasn't smooth or pretty sometimes, mind you. The kids in my school weren't welcoming. I guess I seemed weird, having no parents, dressing in the ranch clothes Addie sewed, caring more about the bugs and plants than academics. I learned how to play by myself." He thought she might cry again, but instead she turned a smile on him, the sweetest smile he'd ever seen, a smile that made his heart thump. "Your mother and my aunt gave us the same verse. How's that for amazing?" she said.

Amazing. Definitely. He didn't know why he was over-the-moon grateful that he'd shared the memory. A God thing, as his mom used to say. Too bad he didn't let more of those God things out of his mouth. Might be less room for his foot.

She nodded. "Eyes up, not down. I like the way your mom put it."

"Me, too."

Judging by her more relaxed demeanor, her spirits were lighter by the time they arrived at the ranch. So were his.

At the ranch, he checked with Alex, Phil and Quinn, none of whom had a theory on how Terrence had known they'd be at the store. Then he went into the living room with Ella and joined the scheduled Zoom meeting to report in.

Lorenza's normally serious face grew downright grave as she listened. "He's getting too close."

"I agree." Brayden outlined the safety precautions he'd taken on the ranch. "But I could use help trying to canvass the area. There's too much wilderness where Terrence could have hidden those reindeer for me to search by myself. And that might be the key to finding him. If Katie's theory is right, he's not feeding them well, but at least we can assume he hasn't killed them. Yet."

Maya Rodriquez unmuted her microphone and spoke up, pausing for a moment when her Malinois, Sarge, poked his nose at the screen. She flipped her dark braid over her shoulder.

"Sarge and I will see what we can find. He couldn't have taken them too far out of Palmer if he's in town buying supplies for them."

Brayden nodded. "He's holed up somewhere, likely a place with a fenced field or a corral."

Maya nodded. "We're on it."

Brayden thanked her. "And an extra person tomorrow for the Christmas Fair meeting wouldn't hurt, either. We've got fourteen people coming, and I'm concerned about the forested property and the riverbed. Both weak points for security."

"I can do it," Gabriel said. "I—"

"One moment," the colonel said, looking at her phone. "I just got a text from Poppy."

Brayden took a breath. Poppy and her wolfhound had been combing the wild acres of Chugach, searching for any sign of Cole Seaver, Eli's godmother's missing son. Brayden had met Bettina Seaver at a police family gathering several years prior. He'd liked her intense blue eyes and the impish smile she reserved for her godson Eli. Eli explained how pained she was when her son became more and more enamored with the wilderness until he cut all ties with his old life and simply disappeared. Rumor was he lived in a remote off-the-grid homestead with a wife and child.

Bettina was struggling with stage four can-

cer, and Eli wanted to grant her wish for a re-
union with her son before she passed. How
would that feel, he wondered, to have someone you loved with your whole being removed
from your life without a word? It had been
hard enough on him to have his father walk
out when he was twelve.

"Why did Dad leave?" he'd asked his mother
again and again.

"He got tired of it all," she'd snapped one
time in exasperation at his repeated question.

Tired of him? He'd wondered if he'd gotten better grades, been the star on the baseball
team, shared his father's interest in ham ra-
dios… The adult in him realized he wasn't to
blame for his father's departure, but some part
of him deep down worried that maybe he just
wasn't enough. Jamie must have thought so.

Too old…too straitlaced.

He flashed briefly on Katie. Did she feel that
way, too? He was eight years older. Was he also
too one-note, too bland outside his trooper iden-
tity to warrant interest? And why did he wonder about that, anyway?

Pay attention. He held his breath while waiting for Lorenza to share the text. Had Cole
Seaver been found?

"Poppy says she encountered a teenage male,

declined to give his name, but he claims to know the Seaver family."

"Finally," Brayden said, resisting the urge to whoop with excitement. "Where?"

The colonel continued. "Kid's cagey. He didn't want to give up their whereabouts. He promised to pass on Poppy's contact info and tell them she needs to talk to them."

Brayden's shoulders sagged. "Is this kid even telling the truth in the first place? And if he is, will he really deliver the message?"

"And will Cole Seaver actually contact us?" Hunter McCord put in. "He walked out of his mother's life years ago, and he might not be willing to do an about-face."

"If we can talk to Cole, explain things..." Maya said. "I can't believe he would turn his back on his dying mother."

Lorenza put her phone away. "All we can do is make contact. The rest is up to him."

"We're looking for a wilderness family, stolen reindeer, a fugitive uncle, and we've still got a murderous groom and his target out there somewhere." Helena Maddox blew out a frustrated breath.

The stakes had gotten so high so fast they were all striving to keep up. As much as he wanted to help Poppy search for Cole and Gabriel locate Violet James, he knew his focus had to stay on Katie and the Family K. Had he really resisted the assignment only a few days ago? Now her safety was all he could think about.

They ended the meeting and Brayden listened to Katie's kitchen clatter. She'd started to hum something, a tune he didn't know. Her quirks surprised him. Quiet, serious, no-nonsense, but she seemed to be singing something about frogs in a watermelon patch. Ella's tale wagged as she listened. When the dog lumbered into the kitchen to check things out, Katie put down a water bowl for her.

"Don't..." he started. *Too late.* Ella dived her paws into that bowl and scrabbled for all she was worth until the water was splattered everywhere and Ella was satisfied.

Katie laughed, a belly chuckle that made him smile, too. "Sorry."

"I should have warned you about her level of enthusiasm for water. I'll get some paper towels and dry that up," he said.

After another chuckle, she went back to her frog-and-watermelon song.

If she could still laugh while her murderous uncle was at large, then he would allow himself the pleasure of being near her.

It was an assignment, and he wouldn't forget it, but how could he resist?

SIX

Katie slammed her alarm off and sat up groggy the next morning. She came to full alertness with a gasp. Six thirty? She'd meant to be in the kitchen by six. Frightening dreams she could not quite recall had roused her on and off during the night. Once she'd actually gone to the window, searching the dark acres for signs of Terrence. Instead, she'd seen Brayden and Ella returning from a drive around the property.

He hadn't noticed her at the window, as he gave his beloved dog a good belly scratch. Ella rewarded him by standing on her hind legs, which put her golf-ball-sized nose about even with his face. She imagined Brayden's smile and it made butterflies take flight in her stomach. At least she'd been able to sleep for a few hours after that. Their temporary arrangement was awkward, but it did ease her spirit to have him close by.

A quick face wash, ponytail, clean jeans

and a shirt, and she was hurrying down the stairs, surprised to find Brayden already in the kitchen. He was wrapped in her Reindeer Roundup apron, a leftover from a long-ago fundraiser. The comical cartoon reindeer dancing in tutus across the pink fabric looked completely out of place on the big man spreading mustard and mayo onto sliced bread.

He waved a rubber-gloved hand at her and pointed to the coffee machine. "Heard you coming and brewed you a cup. I did not break anything while doing so, I might add, so that's a win."

"You don't have to make the sandwiches," she said.

He pulled a look of mock offense. "I am the meat master, as we discussed. I figured I'd get a head start. You were on brownie duty yesterday."

She pulled the foil-wrapped tray from the counter. "I sure was. Thirty-six chocolate peanut butter cup brownies."

He became overly focused wiping at a spot on his reindeer apron. A contrite look revealed delicate crow's-feet around his eyes. Surprisingly attractive. "Er, actually, it's closer to thirty-five. I got up early, as I mentioned, and there was the quality-control issue to consider.

Um, might even be thirty-four left because I take my job assignments seriously."

The sheepish look made her laugh. "I understand completely. How is the quality, by the way?"

"I would give it a two thumbs-up if my thumbs weren't already busy making sandwiches."

"Glad to hear it." Unaccustomed pleasure bubbled in her spirit. He liked the brownies. Embarrassed by her own silliness, she got to work. She laid out brown paper bags and tucked the sandwiches inside as Brayden finished them, along with a bag of chips, an apple and a brownie. Pitchers of iced water and lemonade would be prepared closer to the noon hour and placed outside on the long weathered picnic benches. Eyeing the dark wall of clouds that was rolling in with the promise of a storm, she mentally figured on ushering everyone inside if the rain came before the food was finished. Compared with the other complications, a storm was a mere trifle. Alaskans could handle inclement weather without the slightest concern.

Her phone rang with a familiar number, Addie calling on the new cell they'd gotten her. Fortunately, her number hadn't changed.

"Hi, Aunt Addie. How are you feeling?"

Addie probably hadn't slept well, either, she realized, as the older woman's worries came spilling out. Katie listened patiently and reassured her that all the details of the upcoming meeting were taken care of. It required a good twenty minutes of calming before her aunt could be persuaded that she should hang up. Brayden was done with sandwich construction by the time she ended the call.

He inquired with a raised eyebrow. "I take it Aunt Addie isn't comfortable with delegating?"

"That's an understatement. She's particularly worried about Sweetie. Addie got his mom, Lulu, from a family in town who had to move away and couldn't keep her. She wasn't in the greatest health, since they didn't know much about raising a reindeer. I was visiting the Family K when Lulu delivered Sweetie." The moment was embedded in her soul. She realized she'd gone quiet only when Brayden touched her shoulder.

"A powerful memory?"

"Yes. He was so small and clumsy when he was born, smaller than any other reindeer baby I'd ever seen. Lulu cleaned and nuzzled him. Then she got up and walked away a few feet and lay down again. Sweetie tried and tried to get up. He took one step toward her and collapsed. I wanted so badly for Lulu to go to

Sweetie and help him, but she didn't. Instead, she got up and walked away a few more steps and lay down again. It took him another fifteen minutes before he managed to master his legs enough to get to her, and then they both lay down for a good nursing."

"Nothing like a mother's love."

"No, there isn't." She touched a finger to the smooth pendant. "I don't remember everything, but I know Mom was ecstatic to be pregnant with my brother. I gathered they thought she could not have any more children."

A fountain of grief burst out for the tiny brother she'd never had a chance to meet. Katie had never talked about it with anyone, even Addie. She could not tell Brayden about the crayon pictures she'd taped all over a corner of the room she would have shared with him, or about the piggy-bank coins she'd been collecting to buy a two-seater kayak that they would paddle together someday on their grand adventures.

Brayden leaned his cheek on the top of her head. Just for a moment, she wondered what it would be like to share everything with him, the faults and fears and fumblings. But she didn't trust anyone that much, especially Brayden Ford. She clung to him for another second, struggling to catch her breath before she detached herself.

"What am I doing? Crying onto your reindeer apron? Dunno where that came from," she said, sniffling.

"I don't mind."

"I was talking about Addie's phone call," she blurted. "Anyway, she's worried about Sweetie and she won't take my word that he's okay. Not surprising. When he was born, he was so small that we wanted to keep a round-the-clock watch over him. I volunteered to take a shift, but she insisted on staying there all night. I think she was worried I might doze off and miss something critical."

There was still a soft and thoughtful gleam in Brayden's eyes, but he did not press. "I have an aunt like that, too, only her area of focus is senior dogs. This hospital stay must be getting on Aunt Addie's very last nerve."

"Yes, and I fear the nurses are getting the brunt of it. The good news is she might be allowed to come home next week."

"Ah. That is good news."

There was a shade of calculation in his tone. She realized the comment had set his mental wheels turning. With Addie's return, there would be two targets instead of one.

Targets. He was focused on his protective

details. And why shouldn't he? It was his assignment, after all. The embrace was just part of that protectiveness, nothing more. It was a good reminder to herself that though Brayden was certainly not the hard-nosed person she'd thought him to be, baring her personal drama with him was ridiculous and risky. She was a job to him, just like Addie. What was more, solving the Terrence case would be a way to prove himself to the boss and maybe give him a career boost.

Determined to keep her head in business mode, she finished the bagged lunches and put them in the fridge. On the porch, she tugged on a pair of boots. Brayden followed her to the pen, where Quinn was already taking care of tossing hay to the herd. He handed her an enormous glass bottle of milk. "Care to do the honors?"

She nodded gratefully. The truth was, she dreaded giving up her nursing duties for Sweetie. Could be she was more like Addie than she cared to admit. *A mother's love...* It was hard enough seeing the young reindeer wandering around and bawling for his mother. Somehow, feeding him that bottle was an unspoken promise she'd made to Lulu and, in some odd way, made her feel connected to her own mother.

We'll find you and I will do everything I can for your baby until you come home.

Sweetie noticed the bottle and approached with a mixture of longing and concern. She crouched down, having learned by trial and error that it made the animal more comfortable.

"Here, baby," she crooned. "Mama would want you to drink up your milk." She needed to wait only a moment more before Sweetie's hunger overcame his hesitation and he latched on to the bottle. His vigorous sucking made loud smacking noises that left her chuckling.

"Biggest baby I ever did see," Brayden said.

"Not really. Most reindeer babies are weaned by six months, so he needs two months more of bottles before he's ready to completely give up milk for greens." She ran a hand over Sweetie's ribs while he sucked up the last swallow. His sides were warm, his winter double coat coming in nicely. The thick underfur was an excellent cold-weather protection and the longer hollow hairs on top would allow him to swim with ease. She enjoyed the surprised reactions she got from visitors when they were told that reindeer could float like corks and seemed to enjoy their swimming. In the wet months, the small lake on their property was an entertaining spot to watch the reindeer swim.

"He's a blue-ribbon eater," Brayden remarked,

watching Sweetie guzzle his milk. He'd stayed outside the fence, arms resting on the wood planks.

"He wasn't at first. It took me ages to get him to accept the bottle. He's still too thin."

"But coming along," Quinn said, handing her a towel to wipe the milk drops from her fingers. "When I first came out here to show my girls your new addition, he was spindly as all get-out. You've fattened him up some."

Sweetie detached from the empty bottle and skittered away. Ella took notice now and meandered over to him, sticking her muzzle through the wood posts. Brayden laughed. "Would you look at that?"

The dog extended a slobbery tongue through the fence to swab all the milk drops from Sweetie's face. They all laughed, the mingled sound floating away in the pristine air. Ella finished and Sweetie darted off to follow the adults from the pen into the pasture.

Quinn cleared his throat. "Uh, now that you're finished, I was thinking you might want to know what I found in town."

Brayden opened the pen to let Katie out and they all stood together. A cold pit of worry formed in Katie's stomach.

"What is it?" Brayden prompted.

"I was gassing up my truck last night and I

saw this." He pulled a neatly folded paper from his pocket. He held it tight against the buffeting wind. "Tacked to the 'for sale' board they got at the station. I always look there since I like tools and I can't afford new ones. Anyway..."

He unfolded the paper and handed it to her, with a look of trepidation.

Katie read aloud. "'Reindeer, female. Lame. Penned at Yukon Trail Road juncture. Asking $200.'" The picture was blurry, but still her fingers went cold.

"Is it Lulu?" Brayden asked, his big, broad shoulder warm against hers as they studied the paper.

"I don't know. It might be. I can't see the antlers well and her head is down." She fought to keep calm. "There's only one reason you sell a lame reindeer."

"For the meat," Brayden said.

She nodded. All of their reindeer were rescues. Addie had vowed none of them would ever be slaughtered. "Sales of reindeer meat soar around the holidays. What if this is Terrence trying to make some money? Or..."

"Or lure you to a spot where he can hurt you." Brayden's expression was grim as he took the poster from her.

"Yukon Trail Road is about an hour and thirty minutes from here," Quinn told them.

"There isn't anything there that I know of except some old farmhouses."

Brayden was texting a message. "I'll run the phone number and the address. Do you have a picture of Lulu?"

She pulled one up on her phone and texted it to him. "We have to go right away, to see if it's her."

He held up a palm. "As soon as I can do some research, but you're not going anywhere near that reindeer until we check the situation out thoroughly."

She huffed out a breath. He was right, but she didn't enjoy being given commands.

"I'll go," Quinn said. "I can get there and back by the time the meeting starts."

Katie tried to put all her gratitude into her smile. "Thank you very much, Quinn, but I don't want you hurt, either. And I need your help today. We may have to move everything inside if the storm comes in early." A car puttered along Brighton loop onto the gravel road. Brayden checked it against the notes in his phone.

"The guests have started to arrive," he said. "Ready or not, here we go."

Katie stood straighter. Though everything in her wanted to hop into her Jeep and speed right to the spot where her missing reindeer might possibly be, she had promised Aunt Addie she would take care of the Christmas Fair planning day, and she would not turn her back on those duties.

Still, as she saw Brayden putting the phone to his ear, she wondered what he would find. A trap? Her missing animal? Or Terrence Kapowski himself?

Gabriel gratefully accepted the bag lunch Brayden offered him at the noon hour. The Saint Bernard sitting at his feet nosed hopefully at the scent. "Katie wanted to make sure you got it while you're out and about on the property."

"Very thoughtful. I'm obliged," he said, unwrapping and taking a huge bite. "And starved since I skipped breakfast to get over here." He cocked a mischievous eyebrow. "Katie said you made the sandwiches yourself and that you are a vision of loveliness in your pink reindeer apron. If only she had texted a picture for me to share with the team."

He rolled his eyes. He knew his buddy would be sure to spread that fun fact all over headquarters. "I'll make a point to thank her for sharing that with you. Anything in the woods?"

"Not that Bear or I could find, except some old tire tracks. I took pictures. Nothing to be gleaned except that it's probably the way Terrence stole the reindeer and got them off the property without being spotted. Could be he was also watching the results of his booby-trapping from there if he's got real high-powered binoculars." He paused to take another bite of his sandwich. "Good thing you messed up that plan. Still, it's a lot of ground to cover. And anyone can access the woods if they have a mind to and get out without being seen. What did you run down from the reindeer-for-sale poster?"

"Number belongs to a Hank Egland, age seventy-five, unmarried. Moved to the Palmer area a couple of years ago. No criminal record. He's got a property with a couple of acres. Scoped it out on Google Earth. It's a bit of a mess, but there is a pen there."

"Large enough for Katie's missing reindeer?" Gabriel queried.

"Probably. This Hank guy could be helping Terrence out by posting the ad. Or it could be unrelated. I'll check it out as soon as I can." Brayden observed the blanket of clouds rolling across the sky and wiped away the first drops of rain. "Have a feeling we're about to lose the weather window."

"I'll help you escort everyone to the main house if it gets worse. When we're clear here, how about I pay Mr. Egland and his reindeer a visit? I can get a picture and text it to you for Katie to identify."

Brayden blew out a relieved breath. "That would be fantastic. I wanted to check it out, but I can't leave her."

Gabriel's lips curled. "Can't...and don't want to, huh?"

He jerked a look at his friend. "What do you mean by that?"

Gabriel continued to eat his sandwich. "That you and Katie look good together, that's all."

"I'm eight years older than she is."

"So what?"

He gaped. "And she's practically the colonel's kin."

"The colonel has a discerning eye for quality individuals," Gabriel countered.

"And I don't think she's forgotten that I didn't recommend her for the job."

"Old history. Things change. People move on."

"This is... I mean, I don't..." Brayden stopped and tried again. "There's nothing between us."

His teammate arched a brow. "Because she isn't interested or because you are a dork?"

"Neither. Do I have to remind you that the last time I had a girlfriend things went just swimmingly?"

Gabriel winced. "You do win the 'worst relationship ending' prize for having to arrest your girlfriend."

"Yeah, a girlfriend Katie warned me about and I accused her of trying to get back at me."

"Was she? Trying to get back at you?"

Brayden thought it over. "No, now that I've gotten to know her better, I don't think she told me about Jamie to humiliate me."

"There you go, then." His friend grinned. "Stop trying to find reasons it wouldn't work."

"Are you, the world's most confirmed bachelor, trying to advise me on relationships?"

"You're family material. I'm not. Plus, you're a little dense, so I figure you need the help."

Brayden was indeed family material and that was another confirming factor, since Katie said she wasn't interested in marriage and which was why she'd broken up with John.

"Well?" Gabriel said. "I'm not hearing anything sensible coming out of your mouth."

He was too flustered to manage a retort before Gabriel socked him on the shoulder.

"All right, all right. I've rattled you enough, I can see. It would be fun to harass you some more, but work before pleasure. Gonna take a look along the river. See you later."

Brayden watched the other man go. Why exactly were Gabriel's comments unnerving? Could his friend detect the attraction he felt toward Katie? *Was* it attraction? Fondness? A growing respect? Something deeper? Whatever it was, he was pretty sure it was only one-sided.

You and Katie look good together.

Looks could be deceiving, he told himself as he headed off on another security check.

SEVEN

The rain held off until late afternoon, when Katie shuttled everyone into the large front room of the old house. The sofas were worn and saggy, but with the addition of folding chairs, there was plenty of seating. The wood fire she'd set did a decent job of warming the room. Cups of hot tea and coffee were offered and Brayden helped out with the brewing of it, taking extra pains, she thought, not to spill any. Aunt Addie would have been satisfied with how the early part of the meeting had gone. Not exactly a well-oiled machine since she'd forgotten to make copies of the planning packets, but enough to get the job done. Everyone had been given the tour and updated on changes to the herd.

The twelve ladies and two men sat chatting in their smaller team groups. They opened various boxes and unloaded flyers and craft supplies to check their inventory. The volunteers who could not attend the meeting had made sure their materials were ready for the planning session. Charlie, the mustached butcher from town, was present. Katie was particularly pleased to see him, since she'd learned of his pursuit of her cantankerous aunt. Maybe she could slip in a good word for him when she debriefed Addie. Charlie was a decent guy, it seemed, and maybe God meant for her aunt to have a companion in her later life. Why not? Charlie just might be good-natured enough to balance Addie's harsher tendencies. He gave Katie a thumbs-up.

"I can speak for the sledding team," Charlie said. "We are A-OK and ready to roll."

The committee chairs reported on their progress until a fidgety blonde whose stick-on name tag read "Shirlene" cleared her throat. "I feel like there is an elephant in the room that needs to be addressed and it looks like that's up to me."

Katie sat up straighter in the card chair. "What sort of elephant?"

"The fact that your uncle is terrorizing this place. He almost killed Addie, if anyone doesn't know that already."

In this small Alaskan town, Katie had no doubt that everyone knew about the shooting almost as soon as it happened. Shirlene's gray eyes were intense, her lips tight. Brayden looked up from petting Ella as the woman continued.

"I see you have police protection and security, which is why I felt safe to come today, but how long can they stay here? What if Terrence isn't caught by the time of the Christmas Fair? It's only five weeks away."

Brayden spoke up. "We're actively investigating, ma'am. We'll get him."

"But you haven't yet, no offense. He's stolen animals, shot Addie without penalty so far. He's out there somewhere, maybe watching us through binoculars right now." Shirlene rubbed her palms on her knees. "I don't want to be bringing this up, but someone has to. I am wondering if it's wise to have a Christmas Fair this year."

Katie felt as if all her self-control was evaporating. She could not let her aunt down.

"Let's... Let's take a break for a few minutes. Everyone, please have some food." She picked up a small box from the table next to the front door. It was marked Christmas Fair Supplies. She'd overlooked it in her attention to all the other details.

How could she salvage the situation? What could she say to assuage them? Mechanically, she reached for the box cutter in the drawer to open the package.

Think, Katie. Aunt Addie is depending on you.

Could they postpone the fair? Turn it into a spring event? She chewed her lip. How could they reassure the participants that Terrence would be caught when he continued to terrorize her at every turn?

Lord, help me figure this out, before it's too late for the ranch...and for me.

She readied the cutter to press it into the box.

Brayden wished he could think of something to say. The meeting was sinking like a rock in the pond and it was all due to the fact that he hadn't been able to catch Terrence, or even slow him down. What could he say to reassure them?

Ella cocked her head from under the food table where she'd parked herself to catch any fallen scraps.

Katie was visibly nervous, shoulders stiff with tension, fidgeting with the edges of a box. He was desperate to comfort her and salvage things, but his brain felt slow and clumsy.

Ella whined. Picking up on Katie's anxiety? Unusual for the big Newfie. Ella was many things, but she was not particularly interested in the humans and their social dramas.

Katie readied the cutter to slice open the tape.

Now Ella was on all four paws, nose twitching, staring straight at Katie.

The cutter plunged deeper into the box.

Brayden caught Ella's low whine, and then he was in action, throwing himself at her.

"Katie, don't open that!"

He reached her and knocked her away just as the cutter slid home. The box somersaulted through the air, landing next to the curtains. As it hit the hardwood, there was a loud bang. The package disintegrated, shooting pieces of metal in all directions. One jagged slice buried itself into the floor near Ella's feet.

The fair planners screamed and raced for the safety of the kitchen.

He scooped Katie up and delivered her there, too, Ella at his heels.

"Everyone stay here until I come and get you," he commanded.

Once he was assured that they would do as he'd asked, Brayden eased back into the living room to examine the package bomb. He'd never seen one before, but this one was obviously intended to wound with flying shrapnel. Judging by the shards sticking into the small table and littered on the floor, it would have done its deadly job, maiming or killing Katie or anyone else close by.

He returned to the kitchen.

"Did anyone see how the package got into the house?" he demanded.

Shirlene raised a shaky hand. "It was me. I… I saw it lying by the mailbox at the property gate. I figured one of the volunteers had dropped it off for the meeting, so I brought it in." Tears gathered in her eyes and streaked her mascara. "I didn't think… I'm so sorry."

Katie gently gripped the other woman's forearms. "Don't be. This wasn't your fault…and… and you're right. We shouldn't be having any meetings until Terrence is caught. The Christmas Fair is postponed until that happens."

Shirlene grimaced. "Believe me, I don't want to add to your worry. None of us do. A bunch of us have been supporting Addie and this place for years. So it's terrible for me to have to say this, Katie, but it's just not safe with Terrence on the loose."

Katie answered with a silent nod.

Brayden spoke up. "If we catch him, you'll change your minds?"

Shirlene's head bobbed reluctantly. "Of course."

A woman named Barb spoke softly. "Katie, honey, word's already gotten out about Terrence. The fair might not bring in the income you need anyway."

Katie looked as though she might cry. The wobble in her chin made him feel desperate.

Charlie spoke up. "Well, I am not going to quit on you. I will be here to help, Terrence or no Terrence."

His words seemed to lend her some composure. She gulped in a breath and stood. "I understand how you all feel, and I am so very sorry for what happened here today."

"Terrence will be caught," Brayden said. "It's a priority of the Alaska K-9 Unit. That's why I'm here."

On the way out the door, Shirlene hugged Katie. "I really am sorry to bug out on you. It's not fair, but it must be faced."

"I understand. I really do."

Shirlene left.

Not fair? Well, that was the understatement of the century. A man who didn't get what he felt he was due could destroy everything Aunt Addie and Katie had worked so hard for.

Not fair by a long shot.

Well, it wasn't going to end that way, not if he had a breath left in his body.

It took another hour to debrief the local police bomb squad and fill Lorenza in.

When Katie went upstairs, he sat in the dark shadows of the porch with Ella, listening to the rain pounding on the roof. Putting the Christmas Fair on hold would be a hard blow for the ranch, but injury or worse to Katie was his main priority. He felt the responsibility for that resting squarely on his shoulders. Terrence had to be captured. Quickly.

He stroked the dog. "Do I need to add bomb detection to your list of job skills?" He'd already given her a pile of dog treats and let her frolic in the water running from the downspout. The dog was probably a better trooper than he was.

He glanced again at his phone, waiting for a message from Gabriel. The for-sale ad Quinn had brought to their attention might provide some answers. His mind drifted back to Katie and her quiet resolve, the way she'd handled the meeting. Impressive, pure and simple.

She was not the same woman he thought he knew, the young, flighty person he had not believed ready to manage a job with the Alaska State Troopers.

And she'd been wise enough to warn you about Jamie. Maybe *courageous* more aptly described it. They didn't have a great rapport before that, and she'd stuck her neck out to try to give him a heads-up. Instead of being appreciative, he'd not believed a word of it. Instead of thanks, he'd given her anger.

The buzz on his phone interrupted his thoughts. It was a call from Gabriel. Brayden answered.

"Hank checks out okay," Gabriel said. "No connection to Terrence. Here's a picture of his reindeer to show Katie to ease her mind, but it's an older female he's had for a while. I'm no expert, but he says it's fifteen years old and I believe him. The critter's pretty rickety." Gabriel paused. "He's hoping to find someone to take it, or he's going to put it down before he moves in with his son in Anchorage."

Brayden became aware then that Katie was standing there, wrapped in an oversize sweatshirt and pants. He gestured her closer.

"Thanks, Gabriel. Appreciate it."

He clicked off and showed her the photo.

"I heard what you said." Katie looked at the screen, her shoulders sagging. "That's not Lulu for sure. Gabriel's right. She's much older." She frowned. "Poor baby. She needs her hooves trimmed and some vitamin support. She might be developing IKC. It's an eye condition that needs treatment."

He was happy when she settled into the chair opposite, arms wrapped around herself. She looked so young, younger than Jamie even. *This isn't Jamie*, he reminded himself, but the lingering unease drifted across his memory. He'd made a fool of himself about his former girlfriend, and she'd completely manipulated him. How could he have been so gullible? He cleared his throat and got to his feet.

"I'd better get Ella settled in at the bunkhouse before I check in with Alex. He's doing the night shift."

She nodded distractedly.

"Lock the door behind me, okay?"

"Yes." Still he knew her mind was far away.

"I…" He wanted to tell her how sorry he was for ever thinking she lacked the skills to work for the department, but when she looked at him with those soulful eyes, he forgot how to string words together. "Uh, I… Good night."

And then he was out the door, lashed by a curtain of chilling rain. Ella began to romp in clownish circles as she did anytime she was around moisture, trying to capture the droplets in her mouth.

"Stay out of that," he yelled. "I just got you dried off from the downspout." Too late. She'd located a bread-loaf-sized puddle. The massive dog was doing her able best to compact herself into that tiny pool. Her contortions were impressive. If it wasn't going to mean a lengthy drying-off session, he would have laughed.

"Ella, come here," he commanded.

She didn't, of course. He was ratcheting up to

his "I mean business" tone when Katie called from the doorway. He left Ella to her merriment and hurried back to Katie.

Her brows were quirked in worry as she stepped back enough to allow him, dripping, into the foyer.

"I don't want to bother you," she said.

"No bother. What's on your mind?"

She hesitated. "I have to take her."

"Her?"

"The reindeer. I can't let Hank put her down. No one is going to buy her in that condition. With proper care, she could live out her life peacefully here, with the herd." She bit her lower lip. "I know what you're thinking. It's not smart. We have limited funds and the ranch is in jeopardy. And that after that package bomb, the absolute last thing we need is an elderly animal to add to the herd."

"Actually," he said slowly, "I was thinking—"

"It's impractical, bad business, a flighty decision based on emotion, not logic."

He saw that lush lower lip tremble and it sent his stomach fluttering in sympathy. "I was thinking," he repeated, "that I'll call Hank right now and arrange it. I'll buy her for you, for the ranch. My treat."

"You don't need to do that."

"A gift. My pleasure."

She put a knuckle to her mouth and he saw the shimmer of moisture in her eyes. "Thank you," she whispered. "For not saying it was a dumb idea."

"No thanks necessary, ma'am. You want to help prevent this animal from suffering and death. There's nothing dumb about it. I'm sure if I ask nicely, Hank will drive over and deliver it here. Quinn and I can unload her."

Katie smiled. "Do you know how to get a reindeer out of a trailer?"

That stopped him. "Uh, no, but I can coax a hundred-pound dog in and out of the back seat of my car, so how different could it be?"

"About two hundred pounds different. I can help unload her." She held up a palm to stop his comment. "I promise I will wait patiently behind the gate, all safe and sound."

He hesitated, thinking it through. The thought of her being there, seeing her face when he rode in with the poor animal, made a note trill inside his heart. He blinked and scrubbed a hand over his damp hair to steady himself. "I'll make the call right now."

He had his answer in a matter of moments.

"Hank's real eager to off-load the animal," he told her. "He'll have her here at first light, and he's even throwing in the trailer as a bonus."

"That's fantastic."

And then she reached out and hugged him, a friendly squeeze, then a quick kiss on the cheek that sent his pulse skittering. How could any woman's lips be so incredibly soft?

"Thank you, Brayden. I understand this isn't practical, but now I can sleep tonight, knowing that sweet girl will not be put down."

"Aw, well, you know, you're welcome," he said gruffly. "It's the least I could do after such a rotten afternoon. So, uh, I'll try to get my dog out of the water now. See you in the morning."

She nodded and closed the door.

As he eyed Ella's unfettered rejoicing, he felt an unexpected rush of something vaguely similar.

Katie had a moment of relief from the terror of her life. And he'd helped. It shouldn't be a reason for the odd feeling in his heart, but nevertheless, it was.

"Come on, Ella. I need some sleep."

The soggy dog finally pulled herself from the water and followed Brayden back to the bunkhouse, both of their steps light.

EIGHT

Katie was ready by sunup. She hoped a harness, blanket and a handful of green leafy treats would be enough to coax the old reindeer out of the trailer and into a pen. It might not be an easy task if the animal hadn't been transported for a while. Quinn would set up a comfortable stall near the other animals, but separate until it was clear she would not spread any diseases to the herd. Hank had told Brayden the animal's name was Tulip.

All right, Tulip. This is going to be your forever home, in spite of Terrence.

Trying very hard not to think about the package that had exploded in the living room only hours before, she went to brew the coffee. She was finished with her first cup when Brayden joined her. He squinted, bleary-eyed.

"How can you look so chipper this early?" he said.

"Because we're bringing home a bouncing baby reindeer."

He drank from the coffee cup she handed him. "Not exactly a baby."

"But a new addition, nonetheless. Are you ready? Gabriel texted me they'll be at the front gate soon." She paused. "Hold on." If she hadn't been in a state of excitement, she might not have had the courage to reach up and smooth down the section of his hair that stood up at the temple. Her fingers brushed his jaw and she felt an electric spark. Quickly, she pulled her hand away. "There. All set."

"Thank you. Ella, stay with Katie, okay?"

Katie settled Ella into her Jeep and drove to the dock entrance, stopping well behind the fencing, as Brayden specified. She waved to Alex, who parked his vehicle next to hers as extra security. Brayden left to meet Hank at the ranch entrance at the end of the frontage road that paralleled the river. With the animal in tow, he'd drive the trailer to the dock gate and they'd cut through the pasture to the penned area where the new reindeer would be quarantined.

She sat with the windows rolled down, listening to the sound of the rushing water. It seemed like a lifetime ago since Ella had pulled her aunt out of those treacherous waves. The thought of

Terrence being out there somewhere, waiting for another chance to strike, made her temples pound. The drive to the front of the property was several miles, so she couldn't see Brayden until he drove up, the ranch pickup now towing Hank's small trailer. Katie reached out and ran her fingers through Ella's dense fur, waiting.

"He's almost here," she whispered.

When Brayden got close enough, she could see him grinning as he guided the truck and trailer. It warmed her heart again to consider how he'd helped make this rescue a reality, a gift she would always remember. At times, it felt as if he had as much love for the Family K and its inhabitants as she did.

In a blink, everything changed. A shot rang out from the shrubs at the other side of the river. The first bullet hit something metallic. She was not sure what. The second must have exploded the truck's tire, because it skidded out of control.

She could hear Alex shouting into the radio, *"Shots fired!"*

Her body felt numb with terror, immobilized.

In a matter of moments, Gabriel's trooper vehicle flew onto the frontage road, siren wailing.

Alex yelled at her, "Get down."

She scrunched below the dashboard, encouraging Ella to do the same, until the shooting stopped and Gabriel's siren faded into the distance as he pursued the perpetrator. Desperate to see what had happened to Brayden, she risked a look. Horrified, she found that the truck had flipped on its side and was sliding down into the Frontier River, towing the animal trailer behind it.

Had Brayden gotten out?

Alex clicked off his radio. "Gabriel's chasing Terrence down the access road. Terrence is on a motorcycle."

If Terrence was speeding away from the destruction he'd just caused, then he wasn't close enough to be a threat anymore.

And Brayden needed help.

She flung open the door and she and Ella raced through the gate and straight to the edge of the water.

Brayden tried to regain his equilibrium, but his senses were spinning. The truck was nose down in the river, filling rapidly through the shattered front window. And the trailer had toppled, too. As far as he could tell, he hadn't been shot, unless the adrenaline and the shock were camouflaging the pain.

Get out. Get to Katie. He reached for his seat belt and released it. Water rushed in, pushing against him. He shoved at the door, but found it jammed. Three vicious smacks with his shoulder did no good. He wasn't getting out that way.

He began trying to smash out the rest of the front glass, but the pressure of the water prevented it. Stopping for a moment, he reconsidered. Waves were splashing at his chest now, numbing him quickly. He searched around for something else to use to break the glass.

Katie appeared out of nowhere, wading through the water toward the truck.

"No, Katie." She could be shot at any moment, swept away by the rushing water.

She stayed, searching for a way to get him out.

He bashed again at the windshield with his boot. This time, it gave.

Katie worked from the other side, climbing up on the front fender and kicking for all she was worth. Ella bobbed next to her, paddling in frantic circles. When water began to swamp his nostrils, the glass finally gave way. He swam out, clutching at Katie's wrist, plunging through the turbulence with her. Ella stayed right next to them, ready to intervene if they couldn't make it. They struggled on until the three of them were on the muddy bank.

"You shouldn't have…" he gasped.

"Gabriel is pursuing Terrence, and they're off the property," she said when she could get a breath in. "I had to help you." Then her eyes went huge with fear. He followed her gaze to the trailer that was taking on water. The old reindeer would be dead within minutes.

"Get to Alex. I'll help her."

"I can help," she insisted.

"Katie, I'm not moving until you get to safety."

Reluctantly, she moved a few steps up the squishy bank.

Slogging through the water, he reached the back end and released the trailer door. The frantic animal surged out into the water, knocking him aside. He heard Katie cry out. What could he do? Reindeer were great swimmers, but this one was old and obviously feeble. She was sucked out into the current. Valiantly, the reindeer tried to keep herself afloat, but within moments only her nostrils and gnarled old antlers were visible.

Katie's face was dead pale, hands pressed to her mouth.

Ella acted before he even realized what was happening. She leaped back into the water with a splash and paddled straight to the struggling reindeer. Grabbing the bridle in her mouth, she began to swim toward shore. It was an enormous effort until the reindeer stopped struggling and allowed Ella to lead her back to land.

Katie broke away from Alex, grabbed the bridle and helped her out. Ella shook herself mightily, none the worse for wear.

"Get them all away from here," Brayden shouted to Alex and Quinn, who had appeared at a run.

Quinn took the animal from Katie, and Alex led her to his car. Her expression as she looked out the window at him was both worried and wondrous. He raised a hand halfway to show her, to *tell* her somehow, that he appreciated her help. That he was grateful to the Lord to be alive, and that he was blessed that she had not been hurt.

Her hand went to the glass, pressed there for a moment as if in answer before Alex whisked her away.

Then he bent to his dog, water dripping off them both.

"Ella," he said. "You are the best trooper in the state of Alaska."

Goose bumps prickled her skin as Alex drove them toward the main house. Part of her brain was struggling to keep up. He'd known... Terrence had known when Brayden would be driving along the river. How? "Alex, did you tell anyone about our plans?"

The security guard shot her an offended look

in the rearview. "No, ma'am. I did not," he said as they pulled up the drive.

She moved to get out, but he stopped her.

"Brayden said to wait. He wants to check the house cameras."

Katie was shivering in spite of the roaring car heater, and she was anxious to grab dry clothes and help Quinn get the reindeer settled in. Surely Terrence couldn't be wreaking havoc at the house when he'd just been chased off the property. Then again, he seemed to be everywhere.

She saw Brayden arrive on foot and run up to the porch with Ella.

He was soaking wet, and she saw his shoulders slump.

She waited until she could not stand it anymore. Rolling down the window, she called out, "Brayden, what is it?"

Slowly, he walked over and turned the cell screen around so she could see.

"I'm sorry, Katie," he said.

He felt the sting of failure as he showed her the photo taken from the camera at the main house. The grainy image revealed Terrence on the porch, as he plunged a knife through the wood of the front door fifteen minutes before he'd taken cover in the trees and shot the tires of the ranch truck. He'd known Brayden couldn't be checking the camera and meeting Hank at the same time. Then he'd jogged off, heading for the direction of the riverbank, ready to kill him or Katie if Brayden hadn't insisted she stay well back from the dock.

It galled him, leaving every nerve in his body sizzling with anger. He left Katie in Alex's vehicle and strode to the front door again, taking pictures with his phone. As he stood there, he heard Katie approach. She was not content to sit in the truck, shielded from the truth, and he didn't have the energy to argue with her. She came close enough to see it for herself, the knife cleaving the wood, pinning a note there.

Get off my ranch.

He imagined the rest of the threat was probably clear to Katie as it was to him.

...or I'll kill you.

She didn't say anything. He watched her absorb it all. Her profile was troubled, but with a resolve in the tilt of her chin. It hit him that five months before he'd been involved with Jamie, concerned about which restaurants to take her to, sights they could see, events she might enjoy that would be worth telling her friends about. So much of their relationship seemed to have been focused on entertainment. It all seemed so frivolous and unimportant now as he took in the woman in front of him.

Katie was passionate about things that mattered—her family, her animals. The stand-offishness he'd sensed was self-protection concealing an exceptionally tender heart. Brayden wondered at the realization until he brought his brain back to heel and asked Katie to stay on the porch.

He sent a text to Alex. I've got this. Take another loop around the property and report back.

On it, Alex confirmed, then drove off as Quinn approached at a jog.

"Got her in the isolation pen. So far, she looks a little shocky, but Doc Jake should be here any minute." He eyed the knife. "You two, uh, okay?"

"Yeah. Give me a minute to check the house."

Quinn nodded. He understood and took up position next to Katie.

Brayden took Ella inside, more for her nose than anything else, though it was clear that Terrence had left. The situation could have been tragic. He wasn't going to make any more careless errors like the one he'd made in allowing Katie to be too close to the dock entrance.

He cleared the house, room by room, as a

precaution, but the camera footage was sufficient. Terrence had not entered. *This time.* He let Katie in. Quinn brought him a set of dry clothes from the bunkhouse and a towel to dry Ella. Brayden stewed on everything that had transpired as Katie changed her clothes, all business as she emerged, beelining for the front door.

"Where are you going?" He shook his head. "Never mind. I know. I'll go with you."

She nodded. "I saw Dr. Jake's van pull up. I want to be there for her exam. Quinn's coming, too."

"Katie…" he started, reaching for her. "Thank you. For helping me get out of the truck."

She smiled. "You're welcome. Ella would never have forgiven me if I let you drown."

Her spirit and resilience astonished him. "I can't figure out how he's tracking our every move. That wasn't a spontaneous act. He knew I was driving to get the reindeer and when."

"Do you think Hank tipped off Terrence?"

Exactly the problem he'd been wrestling with. "I trust Gabriel's assessment that there was no connection between the two, but it's possible he missed something. Or there's some other way Terrence is anticipating our moves."

"My aunt said he wouldn't stop." Her self-possession gave way to fear that she couldn't completely hide. She sighed, a sound so long and filled with despair that he could not resist pulling her into a hug. He held her to his chest, reveling in her closeness, wondering at his own craving to be near her, to make her world better. But he *hadn't*. Clearing his throat, he released her.

"As I said, I never should have let you wait for me near the dock."

Her chin went up. "I'm a grown woman, Brayden. You don't 'let' me do anything. I chose to go because I didn't believe there was any threat, either, so you can't take all the blame."

He wished he could let himself off the hook as easily as she did. "I'm the trooper and that's my duty here, to keep you safe. The colonel entrusted me to handle this case."

Something shuttered in Katie's face. "I will try not to get in the way of your duty, Brayden. I know how much your job means to you."

And then she was out the door, leaving him with his mouth open, trying to figure out how he'd once again said the wrong thing.

Terrence had somehow outsmarted him, knowing their comings and goings. Teeth gritted, he decided that he was going to solve that mystery if it took him the rest of the day and night. It was his sworn duty to protect Katie, and he was going to do his job. No homicidal maniac was going to stop him.

NINE

Brayden patrolled every square inch of the property himself, in addition to sending Phil out on another set of patrols to back up Alex. As much as he'd dreaded telling the K-9 team what had happened, he'd reported in and now some of his fellow troopers were on their way to help scour the property. Brayden had already coned off the road and photographed the submerged truck and trailer in which he and Tulip had almost drowned.

His foul mood grew darker as the day wore on. And by late afternoon, he returned tired and hungry to his starting point, the Frontier River gate that led out to the dock. He let himself through, hoping standing at that vantage point, alone with his thoughts, would reset his peace of mind.

When the cold wind started to freeze him an inch at a time, he climbed below where the pilings were buried in the riverbank. The shallow area was rocky and there was enough exposed surface that he could stay out of the water. Nothing unusual on the massive wood posts.

"No swimming," he firmly told Ella, who was staring with a familiar excitement at the rippling water. She flopped dejectedly onto the wet bank and gave him the "you are a crotchety old man" stare. He guessed he was, too. His back ached from driving the property, and the knee injury he'd gotten on a drunk-and-disorderly call back in the day before he became a K-9 handler throbbed. If he wasn't a good trooper, then what was left in his life? No wife, kids, no hobbies even, unless dog grooming and planting vegetables that died a slow death counted. He shut off the self-pity faucet. He was an Alaska State Trooper, and a good one, too. He wasn't about to bungle things now.

And why was this case, this *duty*, so very personal to him all of a sudden? He wasn't sure Katie felt much more than neutral toward him, and he'd felt no real rapport with her, either... until he'd landed on this out-of-the-way ranch. Then something changed. Was it her? Or him?

He looked down to find Ella slowly commando crawling toward the water.

"Stop right there," he called. She flapped her ears and returned to him. Figuring he could dissuade her for only so long, they trudged up to the dock again, over the wooden boards where she sat heavily at his feet. From here, there was an excellent view of the main building. You could even see the bunkhouse and a glimpse of the storage units. Terrence was familiar with the riverbank, but even he could not remain there 24/7 to track their comings and goings without being seen. Unless…

He examined the warped wood that formed the narrow platform. The individual boards were badly weathered by Alaska's unforgiving winters, sticking up at the edges like a series of snaggly teeth. They were secured to the pilings that jutted up every few feet or so.

Ella found a sunlit section of board and sprawled out to bask. Small solace since she'd been prohibited from enjoying the water. Over the top of her fuzzy head, he saw something that made his gut go tight. Hustling close to the piling, he inspected the tiny item, no bigger than his thumb, connected to a small battery and fixed in place with wire. It had been hidden by a broken bit of board that had once been nailed there.

A camera, he figured. The picture wouldn't be very clear, but it would provide Terrence with enough of an image to see vehicles coming and going from the property and who was in the front seat. It probably fed to his cell phone, similar to Brayden's security cameras. The information wouldn't have helped, though, unless the man was camping out in the woods in time to act on it, and they'd already checked that. No sign of him in the woods or the riverbank.

With a pen pulled from his pocket, he disconnected the battery from the camera. Soon the power would be drained and Terrence would not receive any more info from his spy gadget. He photographed the camera, too, summoned Ella and drove back to the ranch.

Ella was with Dr. Jake and Quinn across the field at the isolation pen, and he would have joined them, but two Alaska K-9 cars rolled onto the property, parking at the main house. One was Gabriel and Bear and the other... He pulled in a breath. The other belonged to Colonel Lorenza Gallo herself. That surprised him, but it shouldn't have. She loved Katie, and after the last report he'd given, she must have decided to pay him a personal visit.

His sense of cold intensified as he got out and greeted them. "Terrence had a camera on the property," he said, showing them the picture on his cell phone. "Can we get Helena out here with Luna to check for any others?" Though Luna was only casually trained in electronics detection, she would be able to sniff out any hidden gizmos much more efficiently than he ever could.

"I figured that might work, too," Gabriel murmured. "She's already on her way. Should be here soon."

Lorenza frowned and fixed Brayden with a hard look. "Let's get right down to it. Why did you let Katie wait for you at the dock entrance?"

Why *had* he? Because he'd believed it was safe and he'd wanted to grant her heart's desire to help with Tulip's transition. What a colossal misstep on his part. He blew out a breath. "No excuses. I messed up."

"Yes, you did," she concurred.

Gabriel shot him a sympathetic look as the colonel continued.

"I'm going to push her to leave, get her into a safe house. We've got officers who can cover that duty."

Other officers, she meant. Not him. "I think she might not be amenable to leaving."

"You are correct—she won't," Katie said, joining them. He'd not been aware of her approach. "Hi, Colonel. How are you? I miss you and Denali."

She smiled. "Hi, Katie. We miss you at the office, too. I know Denali misses all the treats you used to sneak him. The office temp we got to fill in is almost up to speed, but he's not got your knack for keeping us all organized, that's for sure. You've had quite a time here, I understand."

Katie cocked her head. "Both the truck and the trailer are a wreck, but I am in one piece and so is Brayden. Our newest reindeer will survive, too, if we're fortunate."

The colonel smiled. "I'm relieved to hear it."

"And I want to clear the air," Katie said. "I wanted to help with the reindeer's arrival. It was *my* decision to be there, so you shouldn't blame him."

"He's wearing the badge, not you," she snapped. "He's paid to make better decisions than that."

Brayden's face went molten. He felt the same level of humiliation he'd experienced finding out from Katie the truth about his girlfriend. Now here she was, defending him to his boss, no less.

Without looking directly at her, Brayden rested his hands on his hips and spoke up. "The colonel is right, Katie. You should go to a safe house."

"I'm not leaving," she said firmly.

Lorenza took on a more severe look. "Now is not the time to be stubborn. I know you're worried about the Family K. We can hire someone to help Quinn. Other people can take care of reindeer besides you." Her expression softened. "You are not the reindeer whisperer."

"Yes, I am," she said. "Didn't you know? I thought I had that on my résumé." She laughed. "It could be why Brayden here didn't think I was good law enforcement support material."

Now he was thoroughly flummoxed. That laughter. It told him she really had forgiven him for his "nonrecommend" on her oral boards. It released a knot inside him he'd carried for a long time.

He kept his gaze away from her in case he might be tempted to relish the delight of that smile.

Get yourself sorted out, Ford. You're not a teenager.

But he felt like one, hardly able to keep his gaze off her. He stood up straighter, refocusing, reminding himself where his focus should be.

"Fortunately," Gallo said, "the department hired you anyway, in spite of any negatives from your interview. Which were supposed to remain confidential, by the way."

Brayden could only wish they had.

"That aside, it's not safe for you to stay here anymore. If Terrence can shoot tires out and get to the front door in spite of a cop, cameras and two security guards, we can't secure the ranch. Too wide open and too many access points."

Katie gave her an apologetic look. "I appreciate your concern," she said. "But there's something you should know." She wiggled her phone. "The hospital called and Aunt Addie is being released first thing Monday morning. I'm not just being stubborn by staying." Any mischievousness was gone, leaving Katie serious as the grave. "I have to take care of her because she has no one else. I don't have a choice. She didn't turn her back on me when I had no one, and I'm not going to turn my back on her, either."

"We can arrange for her to visit the ranch occasionally, for both of you to…" Gabriel started.

"You've met my aunt, right?" Katie said.

He nodded.

"All of you have?"

Lorenza and Brayden added their affirmatives.

"Do any of you think there's the slightest chance you'll convince her to go stay in a safe house?"

There was dead silence.

"Yep," Katie said. "Me, neither. She can't turn away from these animals and I can't turn away from her, so it looks like you troopers are going to have to catch Terrence so we can all get back to business as usual. If you can do it soon, maybe we can save this sad-sack ranch after all."

Her phone buzzed with a text. "That's Doc Jake. I need to go talk to him. Let yourselves into the house if you want to have a meeting. I'll be back soon." She jogged away.

Lorenza stared after her. "Such a determined young woman."

Like someone else I know, Brayden thought. It was clear that the colonel admired Katie for her strength. Something in her expression made him think she'd not for a moment believed Katie would agree to go to a safe house.

They sat inside and Brayden took a seat facing the window where he could barely make out Katie's bright green shirt, Quinn by her side, as they talked to the veterinarian.

Far out of rifle range, he assured himself. Alex's security vehicle was making a pass up the dirt access road. He would shorten Phil's and Alex's routes and increase the frequency. Call Phil to brief him and rethink the night sweeps.

He needed to make some changes to ensure her safety. Would Katie allow him to bunk on a sofa in the main house? It didn't feel right not being able to personally secure the main house during the night. Better to have his ears and Ella's close in case...

"Brayden? Are you still with us?"

He looked up to find the colonel staring at him. "Yes, ma'am. Sorry. What did you say?"

Gabriel was doing his best to hide a smile. He was probably enjoying the fact that it was Brayden on the receiving end of the colonel's ire instead of himself. "I was explaining that Anchorage PD called this morning. They said they have footage of a woman matching Violet James's description at an ATM."

"An ATM?" Brayden said in surprise. "I didn't think she had a wallet with her, or that she'd dare use it." Violet was the orphaned daughter of a late Alaskan oil baron, so she had money, if she could access it. So far, she hadn't, to his knowledge.

"We haven't had any activity on her bank accounts," Gabriel confirmed, "but I'll check again." He glanced out the window.

Helena Maddox climbed out of her car, long hair pulled into a brown twist. The eager Norwegian elkhound pranced along next to her. The dog was a whiz at tracking people, but Helena had been enhancing her abilities by cross-training in their spare time.

"Hey," she said, as Gabriel let her in. "Sorry to be the bearer of bad news, but Anchorage says the woman they spotted isn't Violet. Same height and coloring, but she's not our gal."

Gabriel groaned. "Violet is another strong woman with grit. How she's managing to remain a fugitive when she's due to have a baby in a month is completely beyond me."

"Me, too," Helena said, "but she's doing a great job of it."

"Time's getting short." Gallo's mouth set in a thin line. "The longer we don't find her, the greater the likelihood Lance will. She'll be easy prey with a newborn."

"Ariel is about beside herself. She's going to be crushed that this latest sighting isn't Violet," Helena said.

Ariel Potter, fiancée of Hunter McCord, had more reason than all of them to want to solve the case. They'd both been at the wedding-party guided tour in the Chugach when the murder had occurred, and Ariel had been pushed off a cliff. She woke up to find Violet on the run, accused of the murder of the tour guide. She'd defended her friend's innocence staunchly from the get-go. Brayden figured Ariel must have a dose of guilt over the whole thing, too, since she'd been there when Violet's fiancé had committed murder and tried to frame Violet. Not Ariel's fault, of course, but guilt was a hard thing to shake. Didn't he know it?

"I've been training Luna on the electronics sniffing, but no guarantees," Helena said.

"She's not an expert yet, so I'm not sure she can spot more of Terrence's spy gear if there is any."

"She's our best choice right now along with good old-fashioned boots on the ground." Lorenza got to her feet and they all followed suit.

Brayden handed Helena the battery. "I'll show you the camera so Luna can get a good sniff."

"I've got to go," the colonel said. The officers walked with her back to her vehicle. "I am going to the hospital to try to talk some sense into Addie. It will be like rolling a boulder uphill, but I'll give it a shot anyway." She gave the three of them a pointed look. "I want to know what you all accomplish here today. Give me a rundown on any new security procedures, whatever the dogs find, et cetera. I'll expect a *full report* before the close of business today."

"Yes, ma'am." The emphasis on the last part made it clear the colonel's state of mind. She wanted dotted *i*'s and crossed *t*'s. No need to remind him. He wasn't going to make another mistake.

His career depended on it.

His gaze found Katie across the pastureland.

And something much more precious than his badge hung in the balance.

TEN

Katie sat cross-legged on an old ratty blanket watching Tulip through the wire enclosure, talking softly to the animal every so often. The reindeer still appeared dazed, but she'd stopped shivering. So far, she had not touched the pile of fresh alfalfa or greens left there for her. That worried Katie. Bats winged across the sky, forecasting the coming of dusk. She'd been sitting there for hours. What was more, she was weary to the bone.

Doc Jake had told her to call if Tulip took a bad turn. Between her and Quinn, Tulip had not been alone since they picked her up. The other reindeer came close to the fence, poking curious noses toward the new member. Tulip's nostrils quivered and she snuffled softly. The others would accept her, Katie knew. Gratitude swelled in her heart at Brayden's generous gift. Though the rescue had almost ended in tragedy, it had still been a rescue and she thanked

God that the ailing female had been brought to the ranch. No matter if she lived or died, she would be surrounded by her herd, her family, comfort all around.

An image of her mother rose in her mind along with a surge of grief. Katie bent her head onto her arms and began to cry. How she'd missed her family with every waking breath right after the accident, and there were moments even now when the ache returned, as painful as ever. And that was why, though she couldn't put it into words, she knew she was doing the Lord's will by taking a leave of absence from her job and coming to the ranch. What happened here was blessed, precious, and no matter what, she had to keep it going. The reindeer family, and her aunt Addie, meant everything to her, but how sweet would it be to have a family of her own someday? It was a thought she had allowed herself to entertain only fleetingly throughout her life. So why now?

"Katie?" The soft voice startled her. She raised her wet face to find Brayden looking at her. Quickly, she rubbed her cheeks on her jacket sleeve.

"Hey, Brayden. What's up?"

"It's getting on toward dark. I came to find you." To her surprise, he sat down next to her.

It was an awkward move for the long-legged man and he grunted before he achieved it. Ella settled beside them.

"Ouch, my knee. Man, that probably made me sound old."

She laughed. "No. The reindeer make that noise all the time."

"Well, that makes me feel better, to know I sound like a three-hundred-pound fuzzy animal." He paused. "You…all right?"

"Yes."

"Oh. I thought, uh, maybe you were crying."

"Sometimes…" Should she tell him about the emotional morass she'd sunk into? No, but out it came anyway. "Sometimes I miss my parents so much it hurts, even after all this time."

"Wounds like that never really heal, do they? Just scab over."

"Yes."

"I'm sorry," he murmured.

"I'm fine. Really."

He did not press and she was grateful. Instead, he looked at Tulip. "How's she doing?"

"Holding her own. The antibiotics and fluids should help make her more comfortable. Doc did a treatment on her eyes, too. The hooves will have to wait until she's stronger." Another pause. Katie sighed. "I'm really sorry you got into trouble for what happened. I know the colonel won't hold it against you for advancement or anything."

"Advancement isn't what's worrying me right now." He looked up at the emerging stars.

It wasn't?

"You know, a few weeks ago, my career path was my number one priority, but lately, I've been more concerned about other things."

She watched an owl propel itself on velvet wings through the encroaching night. "Like what?"

"Like you."

She started. *"Me?"*

He nodded. "There's something I want you to tell me."

"Okay, but I have the right to take the Fifth." She waited, plucking at the edge of the blanket.

"You said you saw something that convinced you to tell me about Jamie, even though you knew it would probably go badly."

"Which it did."

"Agreed," he said. "But what was it? I've been racking my brain. I didn't support your hiring, and we hardly knew each other outside of work. As a matter of fact, you probably thought I was a huge jerk."

"Not a huge one exactly," she said lightly.

He chuckled. "All right. A medium-sized jerk."

"I'd go with that, since you didn't take the

time to know me. You mistook me for some young, immature woman without the skills and poise needed to do the job, and you treated me like that for a long time after I was hired."

He exhaled. "I did. Like I said, a medium-sized jerk at least. I apologize."

"It's not all your fault. To be fair, I didn't want to know you, either. I keep to myself, as you know, and I don't share my feelings easily. The colonel knows me better than anyone, I guess, even the other cops."

"Yes. The strong, silent type." He teased a smile out of her. "So why *did* you tell me about Jamie?"

She hesitated a moment longer. "Because of Mr. Winkler."

He blinked. "The guy who lives in that run-down trailer in Cantwell?"

"Yes."

He frowned. "I don't get it. What does that have to do with Jamie?"

"Nothing, but it has a lot to do with you."

He arched one eyebrow. "You'll have to break it down for me." He tapped his temple. "My gears work slowly, remember?"

"You arrested Mr. Winkler for a drunk-and-disorderly back in May."

"Uh-huh. I remember. Didn't have much

choice. He almost walked into the side of my squad car and he had a fit when I arrested him."

"Right. I was at the county jail doing some business for the colonel when you turned him over to the jailer. I heard him when he was being booked. He was distraught because he kept three elderly dogs and they would be hungry and worried if he didn't come home."

Brayden looked away. "Uh-huh."

"And you took those dogs food. And stayed the night with them, didn't you?"

Brayden was suddenly fascinated by the horizon. "Oh, now, that could be. It was a while ago."

She pressed on. "People say that you still bring Mr. Winkler bags of food sometimes at the end of the month when he runs short of funds."

Now he was squirming. "People say that, huh?"

"Yes, they do."

"Hmm. I didn't know any of that was public knowledge," he said gruffly.

"Hard to keep a secret around here. Why would you want it to be, anyway?"

He shrugged. "It's nothing special and I want to maintain my hard-bitten trooper persona."

She went for a playful tone to match his.

"Well, you wanted to know the reason. That's why I told you about Jamie. I figured under your crusty exterior and your poor judgment beat a heart of gold. That's why I told you."

He was staring at her now, the rising moonlight painting the strong planes of his face, lending a glimmer to his eyes that she knew were the green of new spring grass.

"Thank you for telling me the truth about Jamie," he said. "I never said it before, and I should have." And then his mouth was on hers, a sweet, gentle kiss, light as a breeze, and quickly over.

An electric buzz heightened her senses.

He looked dazed, staying close, as though he might kiss her a second time.

The comfort of his kiss floored her and she felt the wondrous warmth of it, but doubt trickled right along on its heels. What was this thing? This feeling she could not ignore? This kiss?

She was his assignment. He'd already gotten in trouble because of her. He was attracted to adventurous, outgoing women, most definitely unlike herself. The doubt grew strong enough that it propelled her to her feet.

He struggled up next to her. "Katie, I'm sorry. I shouldn't have done that."

"It's okay. Just a thank-you kiss, right? And you're welcome, by the way." Was she babbling? "I'm sorry it all went south with Jamie, but things worked out okay."

"Yes, I guess they did." He looked at his boots. "Helena didn't find any more cameras on the property, but I'd feel better if you were in the house for the night. Do you mind?"

"No problem. I think Tulip will be okay until morning." He bent to pick up her blanket at the same moment she did and their shoulders touched. She backed off and let him gather it up. Her body still felt warm and strange from the kiss.

As they walked back to the main house, she could hear the water sluicing through the riverbed. All at once, another memory returned— cold water, her uncle's face filled with hatred.

Get off my ranch.

The shot, the blood, her aunt still and lifeless in the water. Brayden trapped behind broken glass in that same river...

She realized she was shivering.

Brayden wrapped an arm around her shoulders and quickened their pace. He, too, seemed to feel as though the night had gotten especially dark, the rushing river whispering a warning.

He's still out there.

And he's coming back.

* * *

He walked Katie to the main house, sensing
her tension. Because of his touch? Had he really
kissed her? Yes, the sweet echo of her lips on
his told him it was not a dream. He shouldn't
have done it. There was a boatload of reasons
the kiss was ill-advised. His brain recognized
them, but his heart kept on beating a happy
rhythm in his chest.

Stop, he told himself severely. *There's no
room for a relationship here. Keep your kisses
to yourself.* And Katie didn't want him in that
way, clearly, or had he detected the smallest
measure of matched feeling in her?

*There's your imagination going again. You
convinced yourself Jamie wanted you. Don't let
your own dumb history repeat itself.*

He marched them both toward the main
house until Katie tugged at his arm.

"Too fast," she said. "Your legs are way longer than mine. Can we slow to a sprint?"

"Sorry," he said, letting her go and slacken-
ing his pace. He wanted to snatch up her hand
in his, to feel those slender fingers in his palm.
Stop. They made it to the main house. Somehow he needed to talk to her about his idea of
sleeping in the living room.

As they entered, the old wall phone was ringing. He closed the door and checked the cameras while Katie picked it up.

"Hello?"

There was a pause. "Hello?" she said again.

After a moment, she hung up. "No one there."

No one there. The tightening of those lips that he'd just kissed told him she had doubts. No one? Or Terrence, checking to see if she was home? That sealed it.

"Katie, I think I should sleep downstairs on the sofa. I'm sure nothing will happen with Terrence, but I'd feel better if Ella and I were closer." There. He'd stated his case.

He saw her chin go up, the arms folded over her chest that indicated she was evaluating if the idea was a threat to her hard-won independence. "I… Um, okay. I'll get some blankets for you."

And then she went off to the closet, pulling out way too many blankets and pillows.

He smiled to himself. Maybe she was gradually learning to trust him. "Looks like we're sacking out here for the night, El." He turned to find she was already at home on the sofa, paws hanging off the edge of the cushion.

Katie smiled at the dog. "There's peanut butter and jelly in the kitchen if either of you get hungry," she said.

"Appreciate it."

"Is there anything else you need?" she asked.

"No, thank you. Ella and I are self-sufficient."

She nodded. "I know."

His phone rang. "Hey, Charlie," he said, surprised at the butcher's call. "What's up?"

He hit the speaker button so Katie could hear also.

"I was packaging up an order for delivery to the café and I saw him," he said.

"Terrence?"

"Yes. He's in an old banged-up RV headed north toward Pine Gap. I'm following him right now."

Brayden was on his feet. "License number? I'm calling the local cops. Don't approach him, Charlie. He's dangerous."

"Wait—he's pulling off into the woods. I'll have to go on foot or he'll spot me."

"Do not do that, Charlie!" Brayden commanded. "Stay there. PD will arrive soon."

There was a long silence.

"Charlie?" Brayden said. "Are you there?" He waited another beat, heart pounding. "Charlie?" he shouted.

No answer.

Katie's face went white with fear. "He went after him, Brayden."

He looked at the phone in alarm.

Charlie the friendly butcher would be no match for the homicidal Terrence Kapowski.

What could he do? He saw in Katie's expression that she was thinking exactly the same thing.

ELEVEN

Katie paced the worn family room floor until she almost bumped into Brayden pacing in the other direction. His eyes were glued to his phone, waiting for an update from the local PD. Fifteen minutes had passed since they got Charlie's hushed phone call.

Had the police found Terrence before Charlie did? Was he under arrest and the nightmare was over? She swallowed, considering the alternative. What if Charlie had confronted her terrible uncle? Her nails dug into the skin of her palms. Why did the phone stay stubbornly silent?

She paced another lap until she couldn't stand it. "You have to go help him, Brayden."

His features were locked in that maddening "everything is under control" expression. "Katie, we just had this conversation," he said soothingly. "I can't leave you here unprotected. I won't."

"But Quinn's here and Phil is checking the

property every hour. I'm perfectly safe, but Charlie could be in big trouble."

"I am sure everything is going to be okay," he said again in that irritatingly calm fashion. "The local police are on scene already. They can handle this. We should be hearing from them any minute."

"Brayden," she said, her voice shrill. "Charlie could be dead or dying."

"Let's not jump to the worst-case scenario."

Her self-control dissolved. "Why not? Lately my whole life has been a worst-case scenario." A rising sense of urgency rushed through her. They simply could not let Terrence hurt anyone else. "Please, go. I will be safe. You can leave Ella with me."

"She's only helpful if you get stuck in the bathtub or some other body of water."

Katie would not be charmed away from her point. "She would bark if someone approached the house."

"Katie…" he started again.

"You have to help Charlie," she almost shrieked. In her urgency, she grabbed the front of his sweatshirt. The thump of his heart thrummed against her fingers. "Please, Brayden."

"Charlie is not my case," he snapped. "You are."

His case. Right. Stung, she let go of his shirt,

turned and slammed into the kitchen. *You're an assignment, Katie. And he's not going to risk his career by blowing it again.* She wasn't being fair. Brayden didn't want Charlie hurt any more than she did, but to be reminded of her place in his mental hierarchy was painful. Why, she was not entirely sure.

She stayed there, wiping down the immaculate counter and fixing herself a cup of coffee, which she did not drink. Her mind spun with thoughts of Charlie, the good-hearted, kind fellow with an attachment to her aunt and a loyalty to the ranch. If anything happened to him, it would be because he was trying to help. Tears blurred her vision as she scrubbed an old stain that was never going to come out of the cracked tile.

A few minutes later, she heard Brayden enter.

Out of the corner of her eye, she saw him standing there, as if he was drumming up the courage to speak. She wasn't going to help him on that score. The stubborn stain refused to yield, but she scraped at it anyway.

"Katie, I didn't mean to bark at you."

Still, she swiped with the paper towel, hoping she would be able to keep from crying. Now was not the time to turn into a blubbery mess.

"I don't really understand what's going on here," he said.

"What do you mean?"

"Between us."

There was an *us*? Her heart trip-hammered. "I don't know what you're talking about."

He stared at her, eyes clear as an Alaskan spring. "I feel different when I'm with you."

The words both thrilled and terrified her. Should she reply? But too many seconds ticked by while she wrestled with what to say.

A look of something like disappointment flickered across his face. "Uh, well, never mind. I'm just gonna tell you the truth because I have to get things straight for my own sanity. The colonel called me to task for involving you in the Tulip thing. She said it was unprofessional and she was right, but I didn't tell her the real reason."

Katie twiddled with her necklace. "Why did you let me go to the dock, Brayden?"

He huffed out a breath. "Because I wanted to see your face."

She stared at him. "What?"

"That's the truth. Like I said, I feel different when I'm with you, like everything in the world is better and brighter. I was thinking how nice it would be if I could see your reaction when Tulip arrived, and so I caved. I let you be there, and look what happened."

He'd wanted to see her face. His tentative

expression and gruff, gravelly tone convinced her it was true. The thought stunned her, that he cared about being with her for reasons other than his job. "No one was hurt," she managed. "It all turned out okay."

"No, it didn't. We were attacked and you were put in danger. You know what that makes me? A bad trooper. I don't want to be a bad trooper again, especially where your safety is involved. I'm sorry if that isn't what you want to hear, but that's the truth. I don't want to lie to you, even if it means sparing myself some embarrassment. You deserve the truth."

And then he about-faced and left the room. She stood there, the cleaning towel dangling from her fingertips. He'd wanted to be with her? Admitting it had embarrassed him to the core, yet he'd felt he owed her the truth. The respect she felt at that touched her deep down. Respect…and something deeper?

The world is better and brighter…when I'm with you.

Who was this man? It was as if the old picture she'd had of Brayden was curling up and peeling off, revealing something altogether different underneath. He enjoyed her company? The guy she'd once thought of as a judgmental, arrogant "medium-sized" jerk? She finally put down the tea bag, still marveling at his admission. What was even more difficult to fathom was that she'd enjoyed being with him as well, though she knew she did not have near the same level of courage he did when it came to admitting such notions. Brayden's presence in her life had made things both better and brighter, too.

What was to be done with that confession? Discuss it further to try to ease his mind? Or pretend it hadn't happened?

It was probably best to talk more about it, but she simply could not drum up one single thing to say that wouldn't come off awkward since she did not fully understand her own emotions at the moment. Besides, their focus should be on Charlie, she chided herself. The tension of not knowing the man's status probably drove Brayden's wild conversation. They were both on edge, scared... Ugh... Why was it taking so long to learn what had happened? She began to sweep the kitchen floor to try to pass the time. She'd not finished when she heard Brayden's phone ring. The words were indistinct, but the tenor of his voice made her stomach drop.

She hurried to find him, grim-lipped with the phone pressed to his ear. "Copy that. I'll be there in thirty." He disconnected.

Breath held, she waited for him to tell her.

"Terrence got away. He was spotted in the

RV disappearing into the Chugach fifteen minutes ago."

She bit back her frustration. "What else?"

Brayden paused a beat. "He ran Charlie down."

Her hands flew to her mouth. "Oh no!"

"He's alive. I don't know the extent of his injuries. He's being transported now. I'm on the way to the hospital."

"I'll get my coat."

This time, Brayden did not argue as they headed to his car, but he did insist on Phil driving with them to the edge of town. She hardly noticed as they took the main highway.

Charlie, poor Charlie, was all she could think as they once again headed to the same hospital where her aunt Addie was still recovering.

Score another one for Terrence.

Why did he always win?

She began to pray.

Brayden realized he was driving too fast when Katie clutched the door handle. With great effort, he ordered himself to slow down and unclench his teeth. Something close to rage simmered underneath the frustration. He hadn't been able to help Charlie without leaving Katie. It was against his nature to turn away from someone in need, but he would not under any circumstances risk Katie's safety again.

And why had he told her all that soft, squishy stuff in the kitchen, anyway? The mortification was deepened by the fact that she had clearly not felt the same way. And all that business about the world being better and brighter when he was with her, he thought with an inward groan. He'd come off like some sort of sappy greeting card.

What was it about Katie? Being near her made him spill truths he didn't even want to admit to himself. He was turning into mush, both his brain and his heart. Purposefully he kept his eyes on the road and off her, even though he knew she was fighting tears. *Just don't make the situation worse.*

"We're almost there," he said. "Charlie is getting excellent care."

It wasn't the most brilliant platitude, but it was all he could manage. The Alaska K-9 team had been alerted, but there was not much they could do except get some dogs to help search the Chugach. Doubtful there would be much chance of finding him in almost five hundred thousand acres of wilderness. The coward must have spotted Charlie following him and run him down.

Again, he told himself to slow down and relax his jaw before he cracked a molar.

When they got to the hospital, they were directed to a cramped waiting room. Two women were already there. Shirlene he remembered from the Christmas Fair meeting and another lady whose name he did not recall. Ella gave them a sniff as both greeted Katie.

"We heard the news and came right away." Shirlene teared up. "That awful man, running Charlie down. It was Terrence, right?"

"That is how it appears," Brayden said carefully.

"I'm praying Charlie's okay," Katie said.

"Us, too." Shirlene paused. "We'll have to cancel the fair," she said. "Postponing isn't enough. People were already scared about Terrence, and now…"

Brayden heard the catch in Katie's breath. "We've still got time, ladies," he said, in his firmest "trooper" voice, twined with a bit of charm. "Don't give up the ship yet. Come on, Katie. Let me get you a bottle of water." He used the stroll to the vending machine to squeeze her hand. "One thing at a time, right?"

She nodded. "Eyes up, not down?" Her voice trembled on the last syllable.

Before he could stop himself, he'd pressed a kiss on her temple. "Absolutely."

She allowed him to hold her and he did so, relishing the warmth of her, the slender frame that masked the steely strength that had helped her build a life after her family was killed. The same strength that enabled her to be committed to the ranch, her aunt, her work. This woman was magnificent, and she didn't even know it. He realized she was wriggling out of his grasp. *Get yourself together, Trooper. She doesn't share your feelings, remember?* Clearing his throat, he fiddled with his radio as they walked to a couple of seats away from Shirlene and company.

She sipped the water and they sat tensely on their chairs, Ella lounging beside them, until the doctor came out. "He's got a broken ankle and a cracked rib," the physician said. "Considering the impact, I'd say he was fortunate."

Brayden realized Katie was clutching his sleeve. He wrapped an arm around her, acknowledging their shared relief. God had blessed them once again. Terrence had not managed to end the life of a good man. At least they could hold on to that. She leaned against him, her cheek pressed to his shoulder, smelling of the clean Alaskan air. He made a point not to sniff too obviously. Especially since he noticed Shirlene paying attention to their proximity. He could feel her curiosity, but at the moment, he didn't care. Katie was safe and with him. Charlie was alive. Those were enough blessings for one night.

The doctor continued. "We're going to wait for a second scan, just to be sure there's no head injury, but he might be released as early as tomorrow after we get a cast on his ankle. He's on pain relief right now and needs to rest, so no visitors, but you can see him tonight. Trooper Ford, as I understand, there's an investigation in progress?"

"That's correct."

"Okay, then," the physician said with a smile. "Just give us a while to get him settled into a room, okay?"

They thanked him, and Shirlene and the other woman left talking excitedly to each other. He did not doubt news of Charlie's condition would be broadcast all over town in a matter of moments. After updating the K-9 team with a text, he turned to Katie.

"I have a feeling you'd like to pay a visit to a certain aunt while we're here."

"You are a mind reader."

Best to keep things light. "They don't call me Mr. Intuitive for nothing."

"I don't think they call you Mr. Intuitive at all."

"Only my closest friends," he quipped.

They went upstairs and knocked on the door of Addie's hospital room. He waited outside, but after a few moments, Addie insisted he and Ella come in.

"They're finally letting me out tomorrow," she said triumphantly. "I've been telling them for days I'm perfectly well enough to go home. I can't wait to see this new addition we've got. Will she be well enough by the fair time to meet the public? If not, no problem. I think folks would love to see her, is all."

Katie looked uneasily at Brayden.

Addie's eyes narrowed. "What? Has Tulip taken a turn for the worse?"

"No, she is okay. Doc Jake is cautiously optimistic. It's just… Well, first I'd better tell you about Charlie."

"Charlie…as in Charlie Emmons, the butcher?"

"That's the one," Brayden confirmed.

"Has he been suggesting changes to the fair again? I told him he can keep his suggestions to himself. We are not handing out coupons for free frankfurters."

"It's not about the fair." Katie cleared her throat and started in.

Addie listened, her face growing more and more perplexed. "Well, my word! A broken ankle? And he's downstairs right now?" Her look of concern was quickly covered by a flash of irritation. "Well, whatever was that man thinking going after Terrence? Hasn't he been listening? Why in the world would he do such a dangerous thing? He's got all the good sense of a bag of sand."

Brayden almost smiled as Katie rolled her eyes. "If you must know, Aunt Addie, I think he was trying to help capture Terrence because he's sweet on you."

Now it took all Brayden's self-control not to chuckle at the display of emotion rolling across Addie's face. Her mouth fell open, her complexion turning from white to scarlet and settling on a blotchy combination of the two. Finally, she snapped her mouth shut. "That's ridiculous. You've got your messages mixed up. He fixes up my roasts for me, that's all, and volunteers for the Christmas Fair because he has nothing better to do. He's *not* sweet on me."

"He defended the Christmas Fair at the volunteer meeting," Katie blurted and then stopped.

Uh-oh, Brayden thought. The proverbial cat had left the bag.

"Why would the fair need defending?" Addie asked with furrowed brows.

"Oh, um, well…" Katie floundered.

"There's a concern about safety, with Terrence at large, ma'am," Brayden said, earning a grateful glance from Katie. "I reassured them we will catch him soon."

"I keep hearing that word *soon* and I'm getting sick of it," Addie said. "If you don't catch him, he's going to kill me and Katie, too."

If he'd needed any more motivation, that would have done the trick. "I promise, ma'am," he said quietly. "I am not going to let that happen."

Katie kissed her aunt. "Brayden is going to talk to Charlie now and we'll be back in the morning to pick you up."

"I want to talk to Charlie, too," Addie told her, flipping the covers back.

"No," Katie said firmly, putting the sheets back in place. "He can only see police right now, and you'll chew him out and make him feel worse anyway."

Addie fumed. "Tomorrow, then. When you pick me up, I want to have a word with that man."

Poor Charlie, Brayden thought. He was going to get more than a word from Aunt Addie.

Since he did not want to leave Katie unattended, she joined him when they stopped in Charlie's room. The man's eyes were swollen, a bruise on one cheek. His ankle was wrapped and elevated, awaiting the cast.

Brayden leaned close. "Charlie? It's Trooper Brayden Ford. Can you hear me?"

Charlie groaned. His eye opened a sliver. "Did ya get him?"

"No, sir." He was heartily sick of having to repeat that over and over. "Can you tell us what happened?"

"I got out of my car and sneaked into the woods," he croaked. "Terrence was parked there, engine on. In an old trailer with one of those spare tire covers. It said Adventure Time on it."

Brayden wrote it down.

"I took a picture of the license plate with my phone." Charlie struggled to elevate himself. "Where is my phone?"

Brayden put a restraining hand on the butcher's arm. "Cops said you didn't have one on you when you were brought in, but they're still working on the crime scene."

He sank back. "I was gonna stay there and keep an eye on him until the cops came, but all of a sudden, he put the rig into Reverse and backed at full speed. I didn't react fast enough and he got me."

Katie took Charlie's hand. "I'm so sorry."

"Aw, it's my fault." He sighed. "Who did I think I was, helping Addie by running down Terrence all by myself? I can't even change my own tires anymore since my sciatica flared up. I'm way too old to be a hero."

He looked so down. Brayden was about to speak when Katie beat him to it.

"No, you're not," she said firmly. "You've defended our ranch and you acted courageously because you were trying to help my aunt. I am going to make sure she knows it."

He smiled, but it was wan. "Thanks for saying that. Boy, my ribs hurt something fierce."

"We'd better let you get some rest," Brayden said, but Charlie's eyes were already closing.

They headed to his car. He checked in with Quinn and Phil as well as perused the video camera footage to be sure there was still no sign of the crafty Terrence.

Katie leaned against the headrest. "Why do I feel like we're back at square one again?"

"Not so. We have two important details we didn't have before. A description of Terrence's vehicle and a possible license plate number if we can find Charlie's phone. That's two very big steps forward."

She cocked her head, a wide smile spreading over her features. That smile was worth everything, like a sunbeam after a horrific storm. Charlie was going to be okay, and Katie had gifted him with a beautiful smile that made him feel like not just a good cop, but a good man.

In spite of the tumultuous day and the unsolved case, Brayden realized he was—for a brief moment, anyway—content.

TWELVE

Monday morning, Katie found Brayden in the living room, bent in half at the waist, fingers reaching for his toes. He didn't make it. She was still uncertain about how to act around him after what had happened between them the previous day.

Don't interrupt his exercise, she told herself, attempting a stealthy exit. Ella heard her and her tail wag gave Katie away. Brayden straightened with a hand on his lower back and a flush on his cheeks. Was he warmed up from exercise or embarrassed about what he'd shared the day before?

"Oh, hi," he said. "I was, er, stretching. Sore back."

"Sorry to hear it. Does the stretching help?" It seemed so natural to be talking to Brayden Ford about his back pain. No lofty conversations about feelings.

"Not really. I think Ella is secretly laughing at me."

She smiled. "I'm sure she's rooting you on. Was the sofa uncomfortable?"

"It's not the sofa—it's the hitch in my gitalong. Got it wrestling a car door open for a stranded motorist, believe it or not." He sighed. "Gabriel's always going on about me doing Pilates or some such thing, but I'll just stick with awkward stretching, thank you very much."

She suppressed a giggle as she went to the oven to pull out the casserole dish she'd put in earlier that morning when she was awake worrying about Addie and Charlie. He followed her.

"I heard you cooking at the crack of dawn. Please tell me what that delicious-smelling thing is. And then tell me I am allowed to eat some of it." Ella was right beside him, nose twitching.

"It's chilaquiles."

He raised an eyebrow. "Chil a what?"

"Strips of fried corn tortillas simmered in salsa with cheese and some eggs that poach in all that nice yumminess." She dished up two plates. "And, yes, you can have some. I made extra because it's one thing Addie and I both like that satisfies her carnivorous side and my vegetarianism. I put a portion of it in the freezer for Charlie, too."

Brayden poured Ella some kibble before he sat in the chair opposite her and said grace with particular fervor. He beamed a grin at her after he forked up a mouthful. "I had no idea vegetarianism could be so delicious."

"I'm glad you think so."

They talked about food, fortunately, and Charlie's condition, which Brayden had checked on. Neutral topics. She found the slight tension between them disconcerting, but she did not know what to do about it. As she watched the rising sun play across his face, she realized she'd memorized the features—strong jaw, tiny crow's-feet that framed thoughtful green eyes, the thick thatch of blond hair that had a mind of its own in spite of the short cut, the gentle mouth that had kissed her temple. *You're staring, Katie.* "Uh, would you like some more?"

He was about to reply when the house phone rang. She answered, stomach taut. Would this be another anonymous hang-up? Brayden put his fork down and waited, his wary expression revealing that he wondered the same thing.

"Hi, Katie."

"Hello, Shirlene," she said with a sigh.

"I was told Charlie is going to be okay. Such happy news."

"Yes." The pause became more awkward.

"Um, I felt you should know that we're having a Christmas Fair volunteer meeting at my house tomorrow night to formally cancel."

Katie gulped. How would she tell Addie?

"I think you know, but I want everything to be aboveboard. I'm so sorry, but everyone wants to be done with it and move on to other projects, so we'll need an official vote."

She gripped the phone. "Shirlene, we talked about this. Some volunteers said they would be back on board if Terrence was caught. Why must you cancel right now?"

"Circumstances have changed after this last attack on Charlie. Some of us have to be on the ranch sooner rather than later, getting pictures for the flyers, getting the decorations from the attic to take inventory, building the extra tables to replace the ones ruined by the weather. We need to make a decision as one body and it can't wait any longer. Postponement just keeps everyone on hold."

Katie fought back tears.

"And then if things calm down," Shirlene continued in a brighter tone, "we can always reverse any decision we make."

Another long, awkward beat of silence fell between them.

"I'm sorry, Katie. I truly am. I will call Charlie to get his vote over the phone."

"He supports the ranch," Katie said.

"We all do, but he might not be so willing to be involved anymore after what happened to him. Again, I'm sorry."

She was left staring at the receiver.

Brayden grimaced. "I can guess what Shirlene wanted."

She told him about the vote.

"A lot of things can happen between now and tomorrow," he reminded her.

They finished their breakfast, but she could not shake her worries. She left a foil-covered pan of the chilaquiles out on the porch for Quinn, Phil and Alex, with extra plates and forks.

"Are you ready to go pick up your aunt?" Brayden said.

She nodded. He went through all the safety protocols. When he was assured that no one was lurking on the property, he drove them to the hospital, Phil following until they reached the main road.

Katie had mixed emotions. Though she knew the best thing mentally for her aunt was to return to the Family K, it had been comforting to have her secure at the hospital with a guard at the door. Plus, it would be impossible to protect her from the fact that the Christmas Fair would be officially canceled as soon as Shirlene's meeting took place.

The thoughts pinballed through her mind as they reached her room. Aunt Addie's door was ajar and she was not there.

Panic flashed through Katie for a moment until a security guard popped his head in. "She's gone to visit Charlie Emmons on the second floor. Don't worry. There's a guard with her."

"We better hurry," she said to Brayden. "Aunt Addie's probably chewing Charlie into little pieces." She decided that she would not mention the volunteer meeting at Shirlene's house until Addie was settled and comfortable back at the Family K.

At Charlie's room, a security guard waved them in. They entered to find Charlie sitting in a wheelchair, a set of crutches lying across his lap. Addie, her shoulder in a sling, stood next to him. Her expression was dour as ever, but Katie wondered if she hadn't finger-combed her silver hair back behind her ears. It made her look softer somehow, or maybe she was imagining it.

Charlie waved at the new arrivals.

"You missed the lecture," he said. "I've been read the riot act for my foolhardiness and colossal lack of good judgment." His face was still lined with pain, but there was a sparkle in his eye in spite of the exhaustion.

"And all-around idiocy," Addie said.

"Yes, that, too, but I'm waiting for the part where I get an embrace for my act of heroism."

"You're gonna be waiting a very long time," Addie snapped. "Because there was *no* heroism involved. Your behavior was ludicrous, pure and simple. Don't try to sell it as anything else."

He laughed. "It's okay. I'm patient. I can wait for my hug."

Addie rolled her eyes, but Katie saw the tiniest crimp of amusement on her mouth. Could it be her no-nonsense aunt was hiding some warmer feelings for Charlie?

She glanced at the other woman. "Are you supposed to be walking around? I thought the doctor said minimal exertion only." Katie hoped the misdirection would prevent Addie from launching a scathing rebuttal to Charlie's remark.

"I am perfectly fine, and how else could I come here and arrange things since this silly man has lost his cell phone on top of everything else?"

Katie frowned. "Arranging *what* things?"

Addie huffed and adjusted the angle of her sling. "Well, Charlie can't go stay by himself in his apartment. He can't even boil water and he won't take his pain medicines properly, I'm sure, if he's left to his own devices. Who is going to cook for him and make sure he doesn't fall?"

Katie gaped. "We are?"

A slight shade of pink stained her cheeks. "Of course. You said Brayden's staying in the main house, so there's a bed in the bunkhouse with Quinn. Lots of room. Perfect for a man on crutches."

Charlie grinned. "How could I say no to such a gracious invitation?"

Again, Addie rolled her eyes. "It's not a vacation. There's plenty you can do to prepare for the fair. Your two hands work, right?"

Charlie chuckled. "Yes, they do."

Katie managed not to come off as too surprised at the details, though Brayden looked on the verge of laughing. She purposefully kept from looking at him.

"Let's ask the trooper how he feels about this," Katie managed. "I would love to have you, Charlie, but the ranch is sort of the bull's-eye of the target, right now. And Terrence has already almost killed you."

Brayden nodded. "She's right. My focus has to be on Katie and her aunt. I'm afraid I can't guarantee your safety." He paused. "But something tells me you might be helpful in keeping an eye peeled, and we can use all the help we can get."

Charlie waved a hand. "We have already established that I am heroic. I'm comfortable staying in the bull's-eye and helping out with security."

Katie could only smile. "Well, all right, then. It will be wonderful to have you stay with us. Brayden, can you fit all of us in your car?"

"It'll be tight, but we'll manage." He opened the door to lead the way when Addie's cell phone rang.

She answered it. Her face went dead pale and the phone slipped from her startled grasp. Brayden managed to catch it before it hit the floor.

"It's him," she whispered.

Katie's blood turned to ice.

Uncle Terrence.

Brayden jabbed on the speakerphone. "Terrence? It's Alaska State Trooper Brayden Ford. I've been waiting to talk to you." He began to text Eli, the tech guru of the team, to see if he could triangulate the cell signal. They'd put a tracker on Addie's phone, so there was a slight chance Eli could figure out a general area from where the incoming call had been made.

There was a pause. "I'm calling for my dear sister Addie." His voice was sharp and gravelly. "Is she there?"

"Yes, I'm here," Addie said, recovering somewhat. "How did you get this number?"

"The guy I ran over dropped his phone upon impact. I helped myself, and what do you know? Your number is second from the top. That surprised me. I know he's not a friend, since you have no friends."

Charlie's face went slack. "Yes, she does," he grunted. "I'm her friend."

"Ah. You must be Charlie. Still alive? Word of advice, pal—stay away from my sister. She's a she-wolf and just as cunning. She'll use you and toss you out as soon as she doesn't need anything from you."

Addie's face went scarlet.

Charlie was about to fire off a comment when Brayden held up a palm to stop him. He needed to keep the conversation going to allow Eli time.

"Where are you, Terrence?" Brayden asked.

"Somewhere close. Don't you worry."

Addie's mouth pinched. "What you've done... running into Charlie, threatening Katie... It's going to land you in prison or get you shot. Can't you understand that?"

"Aw, I didn't know you cared about my welfare, sis."

"I don't," Addie said. "But I feel responsible since we are unfortunately related."

"Always the silver-tongued woman," he sneered. "You should have been a politician instead of a rancher."

"Why did you call?" Addie asked.

His tone hitched up an octave. "Because I'm getting tired of trying to push you and Katie off my property."

"It's not yours," Brayden said. "I've seen the paperwork. It's your sister's, willed to her by your parents, legal and tidy."

"It was supposed to be mine!" he shouted. "I'm the oldest child. Mom and Dad meant it for me."

"Careful, Terrence," Brayden murmured. "You sound like a spoiled child who didn't get that new set of marbles for Christmas." He set the phone down and began tapping more messages into his own phone.

"Stay out of this, *Trooper*," Terrence said derisively. "This is between me and my sister."

Addie shook her head. "You squandered every gift our parents ever gave you—money, your car, the savings account they put aside for you. They knew what you were like. Why would they give you the Family K?"

"They would have, if you hadn't poisoned them against me. I know you told them every bad thing I ever did when I wasn't around to defend myself."

"There was no poisoning required," Addie snapped. "You never treated them well. When Daddy broke his hip and couldn't tend the animals when we were teens, you didn't lift a finger. You didn't even come to their funerals or our sister's."

"Mom wrote me off, just like you did. You finagled your way into their graces and got the will changed so you'd inherit the land."

"They didn't trust you," she said. "Why can't you get that through your thick skull? They did not want to give the ranch to you. You're just too deluded to admit it."

"Shut up," he yelled. "No more of your lies, Addie. You'd say anything to keep the land you stole from me."

"Let's meet, Terrence," Brayden said, cutting in. "You and me, man-to-man. You can tell me your side of things. I'll listen and we can get this all straightened out."

Terrence muttered something. "Please. I'm not an idiot. I'm not meeting with anyone, especially a state trooper."

"Well, you're not getting my ranch, either," Addie huffed. "So why don't you just drive your RV into the sunset and find another piece of land to call your own?"

"It's too late for that," Terrence said.

The comment sent a thrill of fear through Katie.

"What do you mean?" Addie demanded.

Terrence chuckled. "At first, I figured I could convince you, but now your chance is over."

"What are you saying?" Brayden said. "Spell it out for me, okay?"

"It's not about property anymore." He paused. "It's about pain…"

Addie and Katie, the two women who were depending on Brayden for their safety, stared at him with unconcealed terror. He could not take a moment to console them. He had to keep Terrence talking.

"There's been enough pain," Brayden said. "Turn yourself in. Save us the trouble of finding and arresting you."

Terrence laughed, one hard animal bark. "It will be over when Addie's dead, lying alongside dear Mom and Dad in the grave."

Addie recoiled. "No, Terrence."

"Oh, yes. But there are worse things than dying."

Now Brayden was leaning toward the phone. "Terrence, listen to me. You're not going to get out of this. How about we end it and…?"

"Oh, I'll end it, don't you worry, but not until Addie endures all the pain and suffering she's got coming to her. Death isn't enough."

The room was so silent, he could hear Terrence breathing into the phone.

"Tell my niece hello, would you, sis?" Terrence said. "She's like your daughter, isn't she? The only person close to you on this whole miserable planet."

Brayden's body went cold and he grabbed for the phone.

"Stop it!" Addie shrieked. "Don't you dare threaten Katie."

Terrence laughed. "Oh, one more thing. Tell Katie that breakfast she made sure smells wonderful. Chilaquiles, right? And you didn't even leave me any. Guess I'll help myself."

Brayden saw the shock that shuddered through Katie's body as the dial tone filled the room.

THIRTEEN

Terrence was on the ranch. Brayden somehow kept his voice level as he called in hospital security to stay with Katie, Addie and Charlie. But beneath the calm, professional veneer, his blood burned hot as he considered what he would find at the ranch. A quick check revealed that the cameras were disabled. Hopefully Terrence was still there. Maybe the guy was bullheaded enough to force a confrontation.

Well, he'd get one.

"Brayden," Katie called as he started to run down the hallway. He stopped and jerked a look at her.

She looked so small standing there, silhouetted by the harsh hospital lighting.

"You heard him," she said. "He wants to cause us pain, all of us."

"I know."

Her mouth trembled. "Don't give him what

he wants by letting him hurt you. I couldn't bear it."

Couldn't bear it? Because she cared about him? Of course she did, he told himself. They were friends now, colleagues. But maybe that fear in her troubled gaze was something deeper than affection? No time for that now.

"I'll call when I can." And then he was sprinting to the car and rolling code three to the ranch property. Hunter and Maya were already there, having been diverted from their search of the Chugach. They'd stopped at the main entrance, no lights and sirens.

Quinn was at the Family K, too, with Ella, brow puckered in confusion. "No sign of Terrence. Are you sure he's here?"

"There's a few seconds of him spray-painting the camera lenses before everything went dark. No way to know if he left again. Eli said the call was probably made from the Palmer area, but he couldn't be more specific than that," Brayden said. "Stay here with Ella until we give the all clear."

Brayden radioed Phil. No reply. He tried calling his cell. "Phil's not answering."

"I'll go find him," Quinn said.

"Sarge and I will search the bunkhouse and the other buildings," Maya added.

Brayden nodded. "Hunter, you're with me.

We'll take the main house. If he's got a trap waiting, I think that's where it will be."

Hunter nodded. He opened a plastic bag and let his husky take a whiff. "It's Terrence's dry suit we recovered after he shot Addie. If he's in there, Juneau will know."

Guns drawn, they crept past the front porch, which held a soiled dish stacked neatly with silverware, the remnants of a chilaquile breakfast. Probably Quinn's meal. They entered the house. Hunter spoke softly to Juneau, but the dog knew what to do. He trotted from room to room with his handler, excited at the prospect of finding his quarry.

"In here," Hunter called.

Brayden ran into the living room, where he found a message from Terrence painted in dripping red across the windows.

MAXIMUM PAIN.

The room had been thoroughly trashed, cushions ripped apart, paintings torn from the walls, mirrors defaced. Bile rose in his throat.

"I'll call an evidence team in after we're done searching," Hunter said.

Brayden checked closets, under the beds and every conceivable hiding place he could think of without finding anything else out of place. He was not totally surprised. Terrence had to get in and out quickly before Brayden alerted help after the taunting hospital phone call.

An engine sounded in the front. Quinn pounded into the house, with Phil's body draped over his shoulder. "I found him unconscious in his car. He's breathing and his heart is beating."

Brayden called for an ambulance, chafing Phil's hand. The man groaned and opened an eye. "What happened?"

"You were passed out in your car," Brayden said. "But I don't see any sign of injury."

Phil waved away the hands trying to support him and sat up. They helped him into a chair after Brayden set one on its feet.

"I'm okay," the security officer said. "Just groggy."

Hunter joined him.

"Nothing from Juneau," he said, rewarding the dog for his efforts with a treat and an ear rub. "Seems like he kept the damage to one room."

Brayden nodded in relief, then called the hospital and talked to Gabriel, who had arrived to help with the security detail. "I'll bring them to you now," Gabriel said. "How did he get onto the property?"

"Looks like he immobilized Phil somehow before he disabled the cameras. Working on it."

"I didn't see Terrence," Phil said, when Brayden hung up. "So I'm not exactly sure what happened."

"Did you start your shift on time this morning?"

"Yes, sir. Like clockwork."

How had Terrence managed to drug Phil without him knowing?

"All right. Sit tight for a minute. We'll have the medics check you over. I need to make a call."

His next call went to Alex, who had done the last night shift. This time he chose FaceTime to connect. The phone rang, three times, then four. If Alex was working for Terrence, he would have to have been on the property sometime around 6:00 a.m., when Katie started cooking.

As the phone continued to ring, Brayden's suspicion mounted. He was about to disconnect when Alex answered, the screen blinking to life. His hair was standing straight up and he wore a striped pajama top. His eyes were puffed as if he had been asleep for a long while. If he had been on the ranch property to help Terrence somehow, he'd done quick work of getting himself back to his house and into bed afterward. A convincing liar? Brayden had met a million of them, including his ex-girlfriend.

"Sorry to wake you."

"I finally got to sleep," the security guard said peevishly. "They're working on the electric lines and they have to drop crews in by helicopter. Noisy."

"Sorry. This will only take a minute."

Brayden asked him a few questions, but the man either was extremely skilled at deceit or he really had no part in Terrence's latest attack. So who did that leave?

The neighbors? But the nearest one was miles away.

His mind pondered the possibility over and over, trying to avoid the truth until he could evade it no longer.

Someone close by was a traitor.

Gabriel walked the threesome to the house. Katie heard Ella's happy bark and knew Brayden was okay. She sighed, letting loose tension she'd been holding on to since he'd left the hospital. Her jaw dropped at the sight of the ruins of what had once been their living room.

"I'm sorry," Brayden said.

Sorry? Terrence had violated their home again. There was nothing he could possibly say to make her feel any better right now. Off to the side, Phil was sitting in a chair, looking like he'd swallowed a lemon. "Are you okay?"

"I guess he drugged me," the man croaked.

A muscle ticked in Brayden's jaw and Charlie put a sympathetic hand on her shoulder. But all she could feel in that moment was that the walls were closing in. Without a word, she turned on her heel and walked back out, gulping in deep breaths, catching her aunt before she crossed the threshold. "Aunt Addie, let's get Charlie settled in, okay?"

She was grateful that Addie didn't argue.

Gabriel shadowed them as they helped Charlie walk on his crutches to the bunkhouse.

Charlie whispered to Katie, "Do you have police following you everywhere?"

"It seems like it," she whispered back. She'd become so used to having protection, she'd forgotten how strange it must feel to people living normal lives. Brayden had become a fixture for her. But Charlie's life had been dramatically changed by Terrence like Katie's and Addie's had.

She and her aunt helped Charlie to his room in the bunkhouse and quickly put clean sheets on his bed. Addie hurried off to fix him a cup of tea. He sank gratefully onto the edge and she realized he was weary. "Why don't you rest for a while." She handed him the new phone Gabriel had brought. "My number is programmed in. Text me if you need anything."

"Thanks, Katie. I am determined to be a help, rather than a burden."

She thought about Addie scurrying to arrange the details of Charlie's stay. Though she grumbled, there was a sliver of happiness in the activity, Katie thought. "You are not a burden, Charlie," she said. "And I am glad you're here. I suspect my aunt is, as well."

The butcher grinned. "Maybe she really will succumb to my charms."

"Who wouldn't?" Katie said. She wanted to smile, but her heart was too burdened.

She tried to prepare her aunt for the mess that awaited in the main house as Gabriel escorted them back.

Addie looked as though she would cry, surveying the damage. "I'm going to go upstairs until you're finished," she said, voice high and tight. "Let me know when I can clean all this up."

Katie's heart broke as she watched her aunt heave herself slowly up the stairs.

"So Phil was drugged, leaving the ranch unprotected. But how?" she heard Quinn say. He stood, hands on hips, listening intently to Brayden and Hunter. Phil must have refused to be transported to the hospital, but the medics were fussing over him anyway.

Ella lumbered over to greet her, and she

rubbed the dog's fuzzy ears, trying not to look at the disaster in the living room.

"That's a great question." Brayden's face lacked the usual easygoing smile. "Maybe he had someone else do it for him." He was staring at Quinn now, expression stony.

Quinn stiffened.

No, not Quinn, Katie thought, stomach clenching. She wanted to speak out for him, but she knew she should not interfere.

"Are you saying you think I have been helping Terrence?" Quinn said quietly.

"Not saying, *asking*," Brayden said. "Are you?"

Quinn looked at the ceiling. When he turned his gaze back on Brayden, it was filled with fury. "No, I'm not."

"That leaves Phil and Alex. I've talked to Alex and his movements check out."

Quinn fisted his hands on his hips. "Doesn't mean he isn't lying."

"No, it doesn't," Brayden admitted. "But he and Phil were hired by my colonel on recommendations. They're vetted."

"And I'm some out-of-work local with a bum knee," Quinn snapped. "So I'm the liar."

"No," Katie said, unable to stay quiet any longer. "No one thinks you're lying, Quinn."

She shot a look at Brayden for agreement, but his demeanor remained rigid.

Quinn glanced at her. "Thanks for the vote of confidence, but I guess I'll tender my resignation."

"Please, no," Katie protested. "We need you."

He glared at Brayden. "I'm not going to work where I'm not trusted."

Brayden stared him down, not angry, but all business. "Quinn, I need to hear from you and Phil. I'm doing my job. Sit down for a minute or two until we get this straightened out."

"Are you asking or ordering?"

"At this point, it's a request."

Quinn hesitated, still obviously angry, but he sat.

Brayden gestured to Katie and drew her outside on the porch.

"Quinn's a good man," she blurted when they were outside.

"It's not personal."

She folded her arms. "It is to Quinn."

Brayden pulled in a breath and let it out slowly. "Katie, I am going to ask you to stay out of this, okay? Let me do my job."

"Stay out of it? While you shred Quinn?"

"I'm not shredding," he said slowly. "I'm investigating. That offends people sometimes. It's what I get paid to do."

"Don't talk to me like a child. I work for the department, remember? I understand what your job is."

He shook his head. "If I was talking down to you, I apologize. I didn't mean to." Steel crept into his expression. "But this is my job and I'm going to do it, and anything else I need to in order to bring Terrence down." He paused. "Can you understand that?"

Deep down in the emerald pools of his eyes, she saw he desperately wanted her to understand. Her upset warred with her newly developed trust in him. She was trying to figure out how to respond when Brayden went back inside. She followed.

A moment later, Hunter and Maya arrived with their K-9s. "Tell me again your movements this morning," Brayden said to Phil.

The man sighed. "Business as usual. I arrived at five forty-five. Stopped at the main house at just before six for a cup of coffee. I checked the cameras. No one on the property who didn't belong, and everyone drank that coffee, so I know it wasn't tampered with."

Katie made sure every morning to fill a carafe with hot coffee and leave it on the porch with mugs, along with whatever she'd made for breakfast that day. She and Brayden had drunk some, along with Quinn, in addition to Phil.

Phil continued. "I drove to the main gate to meet Alex as he finished up his rounds."

"What time was that?"

Phil looked surprised. "Six on the dot."

Brayden nodded for him to continue.

"We debriefed. He left. I started up again. Followed you to the main road when you left for the hospital and continued my rounds until I got the call from you that Terrence might be on the premises."

Brayden was frozen for a moment, chin cocked. "When you stopped at the main house for coffee, did you see anything unusual?"

"No, sir." He smiled at Katie as if he'd just remembered something. "Oh. I wanted to thank you for the breakfast, ma'am. I had a plateful and took more for later. Chilaquiles are my absolute favorite. My sister used to make them for Sunday brunch."

That silly breakfast. Katie was beginning to wish she'd never made it.

"Where did you put it?" Brayden asked suddenly.

Phil blinked. "Put what?"

"The food. You helped yourself to a plate to save for lunch. Where did you put it?"

"In my car."

They all stared at him.

Brayden nodded. "Did you stop anywhere after you talked to Alex?"

"No, I…" Phil stopped, looking sheepish. "I, uh… Well, I did stop for a smoke. I took a little walk to stretch my legs. I was only gone for ten minutes or so. And when I came back to the car, I…"

"Ate some of the chilaquiles," Katie finished with a groan.

Phil deflated. "Yeah. Just a couple of bites, is all." He rolled his eyes. "I'm sorry, Trooper. I guess I messed up."

Hunter and Brayden exchanged a look. "Terrence must have a hiding spot off the property, near the main gate. He sneaked to the car while you were smoking and drugged the food. We'll send the remainder to the lab for testing. I'll go bag it on our way to check for possible hiding places," Hunter said.

Phil agreed to a ride home from one of the local police, after again declining a hospital transport, since they needed to check his car for prints. Quinn stood, arms folded, staring laser beams at Brayden.

"Not a liar, am I? And neither is Phil, for that matter."

"I apologize, Quinn," Brayden said.

He paused before answering. "You were doing your job. But I don't like being accused."

Brayden clapped him on the shoulder. "And I didn't enjoy asking you about it, but you can understand that I'm not in a position to trust anyone. Can we call a truce, then, and keep you here on the ranch?" Brayden's warmth was back.

Quinn didn't smile, but his frown softened around the edges. "Maybe until I get a better offer."

"Sounds fair." Brayden watched him go.

Hunter and Maya were already heading for the door with their dogs to check out the area at the main gate where Phil and Alex had debriefed. Maya palmed her phone, and she and Gabriel stepped away to report to the colonel.

Alone with Brayden, Katie heaved out a deep breath. "I owe you an apology."

Brayden shrugged. "No, you don't."

"You were doing your job, and you did it with respect. I shouldn't have made it harder for you than it needed to be." She grimaced. "I would make a terrible cop, wouldn't I?"

"Nah," he said. "As long as you could learn how to manage a furry tank, you could step into my shoes any day."

He was so gracious, and his manner so warm, she could not resist reaching out and giving him a hug. His arms went around her waist, strong and gentle at the same time. Her pulse beat quicker at the comforting weight of his chin resting on her head.

We fit together, she thought with a start. But she'd never fit with anyone, not allowed herself to. Was this right or wrong? An evolving blessing or a step toward disaster? Hastily she let him go. "One thing is certain—I'm not making chilaquiles again for a long while."

"Now, that really would be a crime."

Addie came down the stairs with an armful of blankets. "Well?" she demanded. "Did you figure out how my dirtbag brother got onto the ranch?"

Brayden launched into an explanation until his phone rang. "Hunter says he's found Terrence's hiding place. It's a hollowed-out tree right near the main gate."

Katie slapped her forehead. "I used to hide there and pretend it was a castle. I forgot all about it. I can't believe it's still standing."

"We thought about taking it down," Addie said. "But there were always other problems to tend to. The thing is massive, so it would require a professional to remove it."

Katie's stomach churned. "It's still a perfect hiding place, not ten feet from the main gate. Terrence could have heard every word Phil said to Alex and tampered with the chilaquiles."

"And wrecked my front room." Addie's nostrils flared with rage and she appeared exhausted.

"Ma'am, why don't you let me clean this up," Brayden said.

"No... I..."

"Brayden and I will do it," Katie said quickly. "Together."

Her aunt hesitated only for a moment. "All right. I appreciate it. I surely do." She went back upstairs.

Katie stared into space, brought back by Brayden's touch on her arm. "You're deep in thought."

"Yes. Terrence didn't just happen to be listening at the right moment. He must have been watching Phil and Alex closely for a while, memorizing when they come and go. He's getting ready to put his plan into place." *Death isn't enough.*

"But we're not going to let him," he said.

Terrence intended to torture them both before he ended their lives.

Through the twang of fear, she felt her inner resolve crystallize and harden. He would *not* win. He would not take away the ranch. She would fight to her last breath.

Brayden was still gazing at her, the resolve showing in his own expression.

"No, we won't let him win," Katie said, holding out her hand.

He took it and gripped her fingers tight. "Sure as eggs in April."

Katie smiled despite herself. "Where did that expression come from? Another bit of your mother's wisdom?"

"No, my gran's. We always thought it was strange, since she grew up in the city and never raised chickens."

She laughed. "Somehow that makes it even better."

There was danger and stress and uncertainty, all mixed up with a mega portion of fear, but with Brayden's hand holding hers, she felt a strong surge of hope, and another smile broke across her face.

"Sure as eggs in April," she echoed.

The police would catch Terrence.

They had to.

Her job was to keep the ranch going and Aunt Addie safe until they did so.

Thinking about Terrence hiding in the hollow tree, listening, watching, like some feral beast, made her pray that Brayden would succeed soon.

April seemed like a very long time away.

FOURTEEN

The next day, Brayden was mulling over a new schedule and routes for the security team. Following that, he'd need to figure out a plan to remove the dead tree near the front gate. The thing was a monster, so it would be a job he'd have to hire out. He was considering how to get that done without asking Quinn for his input.

Quinn was still on the frosty side, but Brayden figured he was entitled to his feelings. The guy had pride and Brayden couldn't fault him. He'd give him the space he needed and deserved. There was some improvement in Quinn's mood later that afternoon when a shipment of alfalfa arrived and Brayden helped Quinn stack it in the barn. Ella took interest enough to have accumulated several stalks in her thick fur. They both returned smelling of alfalfa to the main house.

Katie and Addie sat with Charlie in the

cleaned-up family room discussing Tulip's progress. Charlie's ankle was propped on a footstool.

"She's stronger," Addie said. "Ate some leaves from my hand. She's showing a lot of interest toward the other members, which is a wonderful sign."

"Can her lameness be corrected?" Charlie asked.

Addie nodded. "She'll require many hoof trims, but Robby is optimistic. He's the best farrier in Alaska. He'll have to wait until the spring to do much more since her hooves are hardening for the winter."

Charlie cocked his chin and grinned.

"What?" Addie demanded. "Why are you staring at me?"

He shrugged. "Can't a guy admire his woman's skills and talents? You're an expert with those animals, truly."

"I'm not anybody's woman." Addie waved off the comment, but even Brayden could detect she was pleased to some degree.

While they were occupied, Brayden stepped outside to check in with the K-9 team via a video call. He spoke over the rustling of papers. "If Terrence keeps driving that clunky RV, I figure he's going to have to stop for gas regularly. That thing's a dinosaur. I've touched base with the three gas stations closest to the ranch, so they're on the lookout. But it's way more likely that he ditched it for something harder to spot."

The other troopers chimed in with suggestions on how to tighten the net around Terrence, followed by updates on the Violet James case.

"I found a clinic that is pretty centrally located with lots of traffic, so she might have gone there. They provide prenatal care, but they're serious about the privacy of their patients. Not to mention the fact that Violet is probably using a fake name," Poppy said.

"Ariel keeps sending her texts, even though they come back 'undeliverable.'" Hunter's concern was written all over his face. "She's trying to stay positive, but it's getting harder."

The colonel cut across the chatter. "Full confession, people. I am becoming weary of progress reports that don't get us anywhere. Violet is still unaccounted for, Lance and Jared are as well, and Terrence isn't any closer to landing in jail. I want these cases closed before anyone else gets hurt. These investigations trump all your other duties. Am I clear?"

There was agreement from the gathering.

"All right. We'll adjourn, then. Brayden, stay on the call, will you?"

Uh-oh, he thought. "Yes, ma'am."

When everyone disconnected, he found himself alone on screen with his boss.

"Needless to say, Addie was outraged at my suggestion that she come to a safe house. Are you the least bit surprised?"

"No, Colonel. I am unable to get her to comply with telling me when she wants to leave the main house. Ella and I are on our toes every moment trying to keep tabs on her."

"I don't doubt it." Lorenza massaged her temples, an unusual show of fatigue. "I need to tell you something. Addie let slip some info I thought you should know about."

"What's that?"

"She had to mortgage the ranch property to make ends meet during the flooding we had last spring."

Something tightened in his chest. "And?"

"There's a balloon payment due in January. She pays it, or she loses the property to the bank."

He tried to absorb that new round of bad news. "Why are you telling me this?"

"You reported before this last go-round with Terrence that the Christmas Fair volunteers have backed out. If that fundraiser doesn't happen, it will be the death knell for the ranch."

He sat up straighter. "You don't have to tell

me that we need to catch Terrence fast. I'm well aware."

"I know. I'm merely filling you in on the stakes so you can properly understand the timeline. If Terrence succeeds in prolonging his reign of terror, it's not just another lean year for the Family K. It's the end."

"Does Katie know this?"

Lorenza shifted on her chair. "That's the other sticking point. Addie said she had not told her. She wanted to handle the matter herself."

He stifled a groan. "I'm not sure it's the right thing to tell her now. She's got so much on her plate as is, trying to keep Addie healing and Charlie…"

The colonel cut him off. "Katie needs to know. Her aunt means everything to her, and she won't want to be kept in the dark. She's a strong, independent woman. She can take it."

He hesitated. How could he add that burden to the pile she was carrying already?

"This whole situation has gone on too long," she added.

Way too long. Brayden was silent for a moment. "Colonel, what if we made something happen?"

"I'm listening."

His thoughts coalesced into an honest-togoodness plan. "It's time to force Terrence to show his hand."

"How?"

"By giving him what he wants."

She pursed her lips. "Brief me on the particulars and then convince me it's not going to result in any injuries to Katie or her aunt."

Brayden breathed a silent prayer. And then he said, "I think I know how we can trap Terrence by using a look-alike." When he finished, she stayed quiet, tapping her pen on the top of her immaculate desk.

"All right. You sold me. I'll send Hunter and Helena to back you up on this, but we only get one shot. If Terrence figures it out…"

He didn't let her finish. "Yes, ma'am. I know. High stakes."

"The highest."

They finished the call.

High stakes indeed. Katie's life, her aunt's and now the future of the ranch hung in the balance. *No pressure, Brayden.*

It took a couple of hours of concentration on the front porch to set the wheels in motion for his scheme to trap Terrence. By the time he was done, his fingers were numb with cold. Ella rose and stretched, her furry behind up in the air. It didn't require a dog's sniffer to catch the tantalizing scent of cheesy pasta wafting from the kitchen. He and Ella followed their noses and found Katie putting plates on the table.

"I can handle that job," he said, taking them from her.

"You sure? You spill stuff," she teased.

"I am offended, but I will forgive you because quality chefs can be temperamental."

"That's me. Temperamental." Laughing, she headed back to the kitchen for the food, her hair rendered luminous in the failing sunlight that streamed through the front window. Like copper, or the tawny autumn leaves. If he could pick his favorite color in the world, it would be that shimmery auburn hue.

Jamie had been everything opposite Katie—chatty, elegant, dark-haired, always in the most beautiful clothes and smelling of perfume. All the things he'd thought he wanted. How could he have been so wrong?

Brayden didn't fully snap out of his musings until Charlie and Addie settled at the table, the poor guy landing in the chair with a clatter of crutches. Quinn joined them, as well as Hunter and Helena, who had arrived to help him roll out the plan. When the pasta, salad and fragrant rolls were passed around and grace spoken, he unpacked his idea for them. They listened with rapt attention until he sat back.

"What do you think?"

Addie glared at him. "I'm not going to let myself or Katie be used as bait…" she began.

"No, ma'am. A trooper will be impersonating you, driving off the ranch. We'll have Phil sow some false information to make Terrence believe you're running an errand, but you'll both be safe in the bunkhouse, just in case. Quinn will have it under watch. If this goes right, Terrence won't ever set foot on the property."

"Still…" Addie said.

"And even if he slips by us and gets back, he would head for the main house, not the bunkhouse," Hunter put in.

"I think it's a *fantastic* plan." Katie's face was shining in a way that made his breathing shallow out. "It will finally be over. No more waiting around for Terrence's next move. When do we do it?"

"We'll set it in place tomorrow morning. We'll use Phil and Alex to plant the seed that Addie will be leaving the property at seven thirty, by herself. Hunter and I will stake out positions on the main road, where he will hopefully try to intercept her."

"And who will be impersonating Addie?" Charlie asked around a bite of pasta from his second helping.

"That'd be me," Helena said, "with my hair tucked up and wearing a borrowed plaid shirt. I'll drive your truck, Addie. Okay?"

Addie nodded, brows furrowed. "What do you think, Charlie?"

The butcher looked every bit as surprised as Katie that Addie had asked his opinion. Brayden covered his smile by taking a sip of water.

Charlie wiped his mouth, brows drawn as he considered. "I think we should go for it. With this many eyes keeping watch, we're bound to get him."

"All right, then," Addie said. "I'm on board."

With the plan out of the way, Brayden could enjoy a second helping of pasta. He'd never thought dinner would be complete without meat, but he might have to reconsider. He'd already reconsidered a lot of preconceived notions where Katie was concerned. He sneaked another glance at her.

She looked honestly hopeful for the first time in quite a while. If his plan worked, they could restart the Christmas Fair and Addie would be able to keep the ranch. The missing reindeer would be found and returned home. He was still struggling with the decision not to tell Katie about Addie mortgaging the ranch, but seeing her happy cemented it for him. She'd earned a little lightness, hadn't she? A moment of ease? And hopefully the balloon payment would be paid off without a hitch.

The house phone rang, and Addie hopped up to get it before Katie could manage. She returned with a look of puzzlement. "It's Shirlene," she said. "She wants to talk to you about some kind of a vote, Charlie."

Katie's face went white as Charlie heaved himself up onto his crutches and answered. When he finished, he rejoined them, expression grave. "Shirlene said they're voting to officially end support for the Christmas Fair. They wanted my answer."

Addie gaped. "They can't walk away from the Christmas Fair. Not now."

Charlie fingered his mustache. "Um, my vote doesn't really make a difference. It was a formality, really. I'm sorry, Addie, but they said they made it official." He frowned at the tortured gasp that bubbled up from Addie. "It's okay, honey. We can tell them about the plan to trap Terrence and they'll change their minds."

"No, we can't," Brayden and Hunter said at exactly the same moment.

"The fewer people who know the better," Helena explained.

"Oh, of course," Charlie said. "But tomorrow Terrence will be captured."

"But what if he slips away again?" Katie lamented.

Charlie raised a calming hand. "Even if the Christmas Fair doesn't fly, we'll find the funds to keep the ranch going until next year."

But Addie stood there, stricken. She shook her head. "No, we won't." The words came out as a whisper. She began to sway.

Katie ran to her aunt's side before Brayden could rise from his chair. She helped Addie to sit.

"Tell me what's wrong," Katie said. "All of it."

And then, in tortured stops and starts, Addie told the story. A balloon payment, the ranch heavily leveraged, no choice but to sell without the Christmas Fair. Katie listened open-mouthed. "Why didn't you tell me any of this?"

"She didn't want to worry you," Brayden said.

Katie's head snapped around. "You knew about this?"

He nodded. "Just since this morning."

"And you didn't tell me?" He saw her flinch, absorbing his omission, the shutters falling across her heart.

"Katie, I…"

Addie's breathing grew labored. "That's it. The penny has dropped. I have nothing else now.

If it doesn't work tomorrow, Terrence will have the satisfaction of watching me lose the ranch to the bank and then he will kill both of us."

"No," Katie said. "That's *not* going to happen. He's going to be caught."

"How can I put my hopes in that when he's terrorized us for months? I want to believe it will work, but I can't. I'm sorry, Katie," Addie said. She threw her napkin down and hurried from the room. Katie followed, without looking at Brayden.

The rest of them sat in stunned silence for a moment.

Hunter cleared his throat. "If our plan works, maybe the committee will change their minds."

"Maybe," Charlie said.

"It's going to work," Helena reassured them. "Ranch or no ranch, we have to get an attempted murderer locked up and we will do that. Tomorrow's the day." She patted Brayden's shoulder as she carried her plate to the kitchen. "Things will be different once we get him," she murmured. "Katie will understand why you didn't tell her."

But the look on Katie's face told him otherwise.

He'd kept something from her, something important.

I'll explain it, make her understand.

The breath burned in his lungs. As soon as he caught Terrence Kapowski, Katie would be safe. She could resume her life, free of terror.

But time was running out.

And Terrence was determined that he would destroy Katie and Addie at any cost.

Katie consoled Addie as best she could. She'd never seen her stalwart guardian so completely undone. Addie was no longer crying, but she sat hollow-eyed, staring out the bedroom window at the darkening night. "I am sorry you had to find out that way. I didn't know what else to do. We needed feed, and the barn collapsed. Our truck transmission failed. The washing machine conked out. I had no choice but to mortgage the ranch."

"It's okay," Katie said, squeezing her arms. "You did what you had to do. There's no shame in that."

She gulped. "If I'd done things better, not taken in so many animals…"

"Stop blaming yourself," Katie chided. "You're not a quitter and this isn't over. Tomorrow will change everything."

Addie shook her head. "Don't you understand? I have nothing to pay that mortgage. It will take everything I have to care for the herd. The Christmas Fair was going to bring in enough, barely, for the bank payment. I don't have any more options."

Addie's helplessness scared Katie. "The committee will change their minds once Terrence is caught. And we won't need to be scared every minute about what he's going to do next."

"I pray that happens, but if it doesn't, you need to be prepared. Find homes for the animals, but the older ones…" She grimaced. "Who will want to take them?"

"Aunt Addie," Katie said more loudly. "Stop getting ahead of yourself. Terrence is going to be arrested tomorrow. The threat will be gone."

"Do you believe that?" Addie said. "My brother knows this land, these roads. He's wily and cunning. Do you trust Brayden to finally bring him down?"

Thinking of Brayden sent a pain through her chest. He'd known, and not told her, but that was a separate issue. Did she think he could capture Terrence? In spite of her hurt and anger toward him, she nodded. "Yes, I do. So can you hold on for one more day?"

Addie clutched her hand. "I'll try."

Katie closed her aunt's door and walked slowly to her own room. Brayden was in the hallway, leaning against the wall, hands shoved in his pockets. "I didn't mean to hurt you," he said before she got a word out. "I thought it best that you not know."

"*You* thought it best? What gives you the right to keep my aunt's situation from me?" she snapped. "I'm her niece, her kin."

"I'm sorry. You're already so stressed and I…"

"Didn't think I could handle it?"

"No," he said firmly. "I didn't want to burden you further."

"Family isn't a burden. It's always been me and her against the world. Addie is all I have, all I've ever had since I was ten years old."

"Not all…" he started, then stopped. "I mean, you have me. At least, I hope you see it that way."

She shook her head. "Let's be clear. You didn't come here because you had any fondness for me, Brayden. As a matter of fact, you arrived under duress, as I recall."

"Things changed. You're making this a bigger issue than it needs to be."

Was he serious? Her anger ticked up a notch. "No, I'm not."

He shook his head. "I don't understand this. Did I threaten your independence? Is that what this is? Did it ever occur to you that you use your independence as a way to keep people away? You and Addie against the world. That doesn't leave much room for anyone else to get in."

She could only stare at him, mouth open. Her chin went up. "I don't need anyone else."

He matched her. "I think you do."

"Because *you* know what's good for me? You're talking like we're friends, but the truth is I'm an assignment. You can't deny that."

His hands came loose from his pockets and he leaned forward. "I don't deny it, but my feelings toward you have changed since I arrived. I mean… I thought yours had, too. We're closer now, right? Friends at least? Or more? Was I reading that wrong?"

All the frustration and fear boiled over into a hot stream. "You got something wrong, because real friends, *true* friends, don't hide things from each other. You, above all people, should know that."

His eyes narrowed. "Me, above all people? What are you saying?"

She felt the prick of hot tears. "Jamie didn't tell you the truth and that devastated you, yet you didn't come clean to me."

He straightened as if she'd struck him. "I…" He closed his mouth abruptly. "I care about you and I didn't want to cause you pain. I may have messed up, but my motives were clean. Unlike Jamie's."

"Jamie was your whole world and come to find out you were in love with a liar," she said. "Maybe you learned a few tricks from her." She was aghast at herself. The acid just kept pouring out, burning him, scorching her.

"I didn't expect you to bring *her* up."

"You overstepped. You're here on a detail. That's all."

His jaw tightened, an angry tilt to his mouth. "I thought you knew me better, but I guess to you maybe I am still that jerk you always thought I was."

His stare was so intense she was rendered mute by it. He shook his head. "And I was trying to figure out a way to tell you how much you mean to me. Well, I won't make that mistake again, believe me."

Without a word, he marched away, boots heavy on the staircase.

She stared after him, numb and sick.

I was trying to figure out a way to tell you how much you mean to me.

She was that important to Brayden?

Katie stumbled into her own room and flopped on the bed. What had she done? Yes, he'd kept something from her, something big, and it reawakened all those old doubts she'd had about having the strength to manage her life on her own. But deep down did he still think of her as that flighty, unsavvy girl who was not qualified? Just an assignment, like she'd accused him of?

No, she thought. He didn't. He'd shown that in a million small ways and many big ones. His choice to keep Addie's secret stung, but more because of who she was than how he'd treated her. She'd let him in, allowed him to become crucial in her life, and the price of that was disappointment.

I was trying to figure out a way to tell you how much you mean to me.

Things are better and brighter when I'm with you.

The thoughts stunned her and underneath was the faintest layer of elation. Her own tenderness toward Brayden had not been one-sided. The happy tune that played in her own heart echoed in his. How important was he to her?

Regret almost choked her. All the vitriol she'd poured out replayed in ugly discord. She'd repaid her anger and hurt in kind and dumped it on him.

And what did that leave in the way of the future? If tomorrow's plan was successful, the ranch would likely be saved, but Brayden would pack up and return to the police headquarters at Anchorage. They'd go back to being only coworkers.

You and Addie against the world. With Brayden here, her world was better, bigger, brighter. She would apologize to him, but she feared it would not change anything. He was a proud man and she'd struck out at the very most vulnerable spot in the most cruel way. Her own behavior shamed her.

She went to the window. Dusk played across the hard-packed earth, shadows growing to swallow up the remaining light. Brayden was watching Ella lope circles around the yard. His back was to her, his tall form hunched against the cold. Her heart twisted. As if he'd felt her watching, he tipped his face up to her window. She pressed a hand to the glass, hope rising for the briefest of moments. Maybe he could forgive the hateful things she'd said, but then he turned abruptly away.

Tears blurred her vision at that silent dismissal. Sinking down on her knees, she asked God to help her find the words to apologize to Brayden and she prayed that Terrence would finally be caught.

Tomorrow…

Everything hinged on tomorrow.

FIFTEEN

Brayden didn't partake in the early breakfast. Bleary-eyed from lack of sleep, he told himself he'd been busy briefing Phil and Alex, checking and rechecking the plans with Hunter and Helena. A self-deception, he knew. He didn't want to see Katie. Thinking of her burned a hot coal straight through his insides. He had a brain in his head, he was pretty sure. Why had he decided yet again to love another woman who didn't love him back? And Katie not only did not love him, she thought him an interfering liar. Why in the world had he admitted to her that he loved her? *You were in love with a liar... You learned a few tricks from her.* That one hurt most of all.

He sat in the bunkhouse, staring at his phone, willing the time to pass until it was seven thirty. It would all go down soon and he'd put the Family K behind him. Ella sensed his mood and bopped a nose into his thigh until he stroked her ears. "I'm glad you still have faith in me, El."

There was a discreet clearing of the throat. He jerked a chin up. Charlie stood at the doorway, balanced on crutches. "Am I...interrupting?"

"No, not at all. I was going over last-minute details."

Charlie's smile was knowing. "I'm familiar with those kinds of details."

Brayden realized the older man must have overheard what had happened between him and Katie. He fiddled with his radio. "How's Addie this morning?"

"Resolved. Chiding herself on her uncharacteristic display of emotion, which she equates with weakness. Right as rain outwardly, but I can tell she's nervous." He paused. "The Kapowski women are a spirited clan."

Didn't he know it? "That's for sure."

"But they don't always say things in the most comforting way."

Brayden's gaze sharpened. "What do you mean?"

He sat on an edge of the couch. "I mean... Addie is afraid to trust anyone since she's had to rely on herself all her life. Seems to me, maybe Katie leans a bit in that direction."

Brayden sighed. "True enough. But it doesn't leave a way for people to get close, does it?"

"No. I'm not an expert on anything but roasts and chops, but it appears to me that extra patience is required to weed out the common from the exceptional where women are concerned."

Brayden quirked an eyebrow at him. "Has that been your strategy with Addie?"

Charlie laughed. "It has indeed, son. I had to package a lot of dinner roasts before she'd even exchange more than a comment about the weather with me. We were going on months before she joined me for coffee. But I'm a patient man." He winked. "And I'm willing to wait for the exceptional."

To wait for the exceptional. But what if the exceptional woman didn't want you? Brayden was still pondering Charlie's wisdom when Addie and Katie arrived. He studiously avoided looking at Katie, but the heat licked his cheeks anyway. It felt as if everyone in the room knew how she'd told him off in the hallway. He got to his feet as Quinn arrived. "All set?"

"Yes," Quinn said. "You?"

"Hunter and Helena are waiting at the car. If anything goes wrong, I'll call or text. You do the same."

"Got it."

He thought Katie might be sending glances

his way, but he did not dare look at her for fear any more lunacy would slip from his mouth. For all Charlie's pep talk, Katie had made her feelings abundantly clear. The worst part of all was that he really did love her, in spite of what had happened. Of course he did. Textbook Ford, loving a woman who could not care less about him. Same story, different day.

Avoiding any more small talk, he exited the bunkhouse and let Ella into the back seat of his car. Hunter pulled out behind him. They both passed Helena in her vehicle, engine idling. She gave them a go-ahead nod. With the hat and glasses, and her hair pulled up, she could pass for Addie with no trouble. She would depart through the main gate.

He and Hunter drove out the rear entrance, circling around to the road and taking up their positions a half mile apart. Brayden was concealed in a patch of shrubbery and Hunter behind a pile of rocks. Time dragged on, the minutes crawling by so slowly that Brayden rechecked his phone to be sure the clock was still working.

That morning before sunup, Phil had reported he'd said the words Brayden had scripted out verbatim as he stopped by the hollow tree to debrief with Alex. Good thing Brayden hadn't acted too quickly on having Terrence's hidey-hole removed from the property.

"That Addie is a stubborn woman," Phil had recited. "She's bound and determined to drive into town this morning without an escort. In broad daylight, no less, seven thirty sharp. A sitting duck, if you ask me, but I don't get paid to make decisions around here."

So the trap was laid and all they could do was hope Terrence walked right into it.

He thought of Katie again and tried to shut down that line immediately.

Do your job. Get Terrence out of her life. So she could live it without him. The pain waxed fresh until he heard a car on the road behind him. Helena. Showtime.

Helena drove slowly past him. No sign of anyone in pursuit as she crunched along the road.

Come on, come on. He drummed his fingers on the steering wheel. Seconds ticked into minutes that piled up. Where was Terrence?

Hunter's voice was hushed over the radio. "You got anything? Why haven't we seen him? He'll want to get Addie now to avoid being seen by anyone when the road widens."

"I don't see any sign of him." He radioed Helena. "Stop for a minute and pretend you're getting something from the glove box."

She did as instructed without answering, lest Terrence see she was speaking to someone. Nothing. No movement from the trees or road.

Helena continued on. She'd almost gotten to Hunter when his phone pinged with a text from Quinn.

Guy near the dock.

Brayden's pulse leaped. He activated the new ranch camera he'd installed on his phone. It was at the far end of their range, but he saw it, a man sneaking along the road near the dock.

"Hunter..." he started.

And then to his horror, he saw Addie appear on the screen, running from the bunkhouse toward the man. "No," he pleaded.

Quinn appeared behind Addie at a full-out sprint.

No. No, no, no. How could Terrence have gotten wise to their plans? What was Addie thinking going after him? He radioed Hunter.

"We're blown. Terrence is on the ranch."

"What?" Hunter's question went unanswered as Brayden floored the gas pedal and raced back onto the Family K. His pounding blood almost deafened him. Why hadn't Terrence gone after the Addie impostor? What had tipped him off?

That was spilled milk. All that remained was to catch him before he hurt Addie or Quinn.

The wheels bumped and juddered over the packed earth of the frontage road. He jerked the car to a stop at the dock and ran flat out, Ella galloping along behind him. Quinn was pulling Addie back, trying to shove her behind him as she confronted the man moving fast toward the edge of the weathered boards.

"You wanted to come for me," Addie screamed. "Well, here I am. You leave Katie alone."

Brayden pulled his weapon. "State trooper. Stop right there, Terrence."

Now the man accelerated and, after a quick look behind him, dived feetfirst into the river. Ella launched herself in directly. He trained his gun on the flailing body.

"Don't fight against the dog," he yelled. "She'll get you out." Ella towed the sodden figure to the edge of the muddy bank just as Helena and Hunter arrived, panting from their own sprint to the dock.

Brayden's stomach was a ball of tension, as Ella paddled her way out of the icy water with her rescue in tow.

Hunter and Helena kept their weapons on the fugitive as Brayden holstered his gun and climbed down the ladder to the bank to receive Ella's burden. "Good girl, El," he said. It hadn't gonc like he'd expected, but they'd made the arrest. The dripping man lay on his side while Ella licked at his hands.

"You're under arrest, Terrence." Brayden flipped him over and his heart stopped.

It took a few seconds for him to realize how thoroughly he'd been duped. It was not Terrence, but Phil, disguised to look like him. They were in league together after all.

"It wasn't supposed to happen like this," Phil sputtered, wiping the water from his forehead. "Terrence promised me five thousand dollars and that I'd be well away before you got back."

Brayden felt like he was the one in the water, slowly drowning in his own failure. "You were on the take this whole time."

"Sorry," Phil said with a shrug. "Security jobs don't pay very well."

And then the full impact of the betrayal hit Brayden between the eyes. Terrence had paid off Phil to cause a distraction and Phil had given him all the details of the plan. Phil had been tipping him off the whole time, sharing important information when Terrence was nearby, probably texting or calling with other key facts. He should have trusted his earlier suspicion that it had to be someone working on the ranch.

Quinn, Hunter, Helena and Addie stared at

him with various expressions of horror as they understood, too. The bottom line was inescapable.

Katie and Charlie were now alone and unprotected in the bunkhouse.

And he'd practically left the door open for Terrence to get to them.

Getting into his car, he rammed it in gear and drove as if his life depended on it.

Charlie had restrained Katie from running from the bunkhouse after her aunt. "Let Quinn get her," Charlie said soothingly. "Brayden wouldn't want you out in the open."

Charlie was right, but Katie was electric with fear since her aunt had run from the house when she'd seen someone out by the dock. It couldn't be Terrence. She was not able to see clearly what was going on since the bunkhouse windows faced the other direction, but she'd heard the sirens.

"Something must have gone wrong," she said. "I'm going to call Brayden."

"Brayden is a busy boy right now," a voice said.

Charlie and Katie whirled to see Terrence standing in the doorway. "I thought maybe I'd find Addie here, too, but she couldn't stay put, right? Ran right out like a silly child."

Before Katie had a chance to scream, Charlie raised up a crutch and charged to deliver a blow to Terrence's midsection.

Terrence batted it aside easily. He stripped the crutch from Charlie and dealt him a kick to his cast that sent him tumbling into a pile. He staggered to his feet and lowered his head, rushing like a bull right at Terrence. But Terrence was younger, stronger and wasn't dealing with a broken ankle. He hooked a foot out and sent Charlie crashing to the floor again. Then he clubbed him in the head with the crutch.

"Stop," Katie cried, rushing to help Charlie.

Before she got to him, Terrence grabbed her arm. She fought him, kicking and screaming, but he rammed a knee into her kidneys. Pain exploded through her body and she went down onto her stomach, the breath driven out of her. He immediately began to wrap her wrists behind her with duct tape. When she recovered enough to scream again, he stuffed a dirty handkerchief into her mouth, which made her gag, and taped over it. Fear flooded her senses like a wave of icy river water. How had it gone wrong? Why hadn't he taken the bait?

"It would be so much faster to strangle you right now," Terrence said, voice harsh in her ear. "But I promised maximum pain, didn't I?"

Desperately she tried to get up, but he kept a heavy knee on her lower back.

"Addie will be devastated when they find your body. Poor, poor sis. All alone in the world."

For a second, the pressure of his knee eased. Katie thrashed, but there was no way to escape as he hoisted her up by her bound wrists. The throbbing in her arms was intense.

No way was Terrence going to win. No way. *Come on, Katie. Fight back.*

He lugged her to a standing position. Through her haze of pain, she realized he hadn't secured her ankles. Easing back a step so she was as close as she could be, she donkey kicked behind her, aiming for his knee. The sole of her boot connected with his patella. She detected a satisfying crunch. Terrence buckled, cursing with pain. She ran for the door. It wouldn't be easy to pull off, but she had an escape plan in mind. She would turn backward, open it with her bound hands, yell for help. Less than a foot from the door, her hopes soared, until a thrown chair knocked the legs out from under her. She collapsed with a muffled cry of pain, striking her head on the door frame. Then she lay there with stars dancing in front of her eyes.

Terrence leaned on one leg, panting from the exertion of throwing the chair. He clutched the knee she'd damaged. Anger sharpened his features and made his eyes gleam. "You'll regret that, Katie. Maximum pain, remember?"

Get up. You have to get away.

But her limbs felt leaden and her senses buzzed.

She could hardly get a breath. Through her tears, she saw that Charlie lay crumpled and groaning.

"Charlie." Her scream was locked in by the soiled handkerchief.

"Ready to go, niece?"

Don't let him take you.

But she could think of no way to escape. The room grew fuzzy around her and she slipped toward unconsciousness.

"Maximum pain" was the last thing she heard.

SIXTEEN

Brayden saw the open door of the bunkhouse. Phil's security vehicle, with Terrence driving, had vanished through the main gate with Hunter in hot pursuit. He'd escaped… But what had he left behind for them to find?

"Katie! Charlie!" he shouted as he sprinted into the bunkhouse. There was no reply that he could hear over the pounding of his own heart. He shouted again, pushing in farther. Where were they? Had he been too late? Did Terrence kill them before he escaped?

Helena appeared in the doorway. "I can't find them," he told her. "I'll check the bedrooms." He almost fell over Charlie's prostrate form partially concealed behind the sofa.

"Here," he yelled. Brayden knelt by the man. Was there a bullet hole? A stab wound? As he felt for a pulse, all he could make out was blood coming from Charlie's nose.

Helena helped him drag Charlie away from

the furniture so they could begin first aid. Addie and Quinn arrived at a run. Addie let out a scream when she saw Charlie.

Helena put her cheek to Charlie's mouth. "He's breathing and I've got a pulse."

Addie's mouth trembled. "Thank You, God," she said. Then her wide-eyed gaze traveled around the bunkhouse. "Where's Katie?"

Brayden did not acknowledge her tortured question because he was already moving toward the back of the house. She had to be there somewhere.

He tore apart the tiny rooms, looking everywhere she might have hidden or anyplace that Terrence might have confined her. She wasn't there. He could feel it, though he'd forced himself to be thorough.

Brayden rattled off information on his phone as he charged back in the living room to join Helena. "Katie's gone." They locked eyes as they came to the same truth.

"Terrence took her," Brayden croaked. His brain spun with shock. He didn't have to ponder the *why*.

What would be the only thing worse for Addie than having her niece found dead in the bunkhouse? Having her abducted, powerless to whatever anguish Terrence had in store for her.

Maximum pain. And Brayden had handed the opportunity to Terrence on a silver platter.

He walked outside, praying Hunter had intercepted Terrence. Phil was already handcuffed in the back of Helena's car. Brayden went to him. "Where's Terrence?"

"I don't know."

"You're lying," Brayden growled.

"No. He contacted me only by phone. I never met with him, never knew where he was staying. Never even saw him when he was hiding in the tree, listening in on our conversations."

"From what number did he call?"

Phil shrugged. "A local number. You can check my phone if it's still functioning when you pull it out of the river." He wiped at the top of his damp head. "I didn't plan on jumping in. You were supposed to spot me on the camera and I'd be gone in the woods by the time you made it back, except my knee went out on me and I couldn't get away in time."

He spoke calmly and practically, as if they were talking about the weather instead of a woman's life. Brayden wanted to grab hold of him and toss him into the river all over again. "The cops are going to interrogate you until you spill everything you know about Terrence."

He shook his head. "I figure as much, but it's a waste of effort. I worked for some cash, that's all. He'd ask me to do something and then leave payment in the hollow tree. Told him your movements, mostly, like when you went to get that old reindeer so he'd know where to set up the ambush. Cash, always cash."

Brayden shook his head in disgust. "You handed Katie over for cash."

Phil grimaced. "I was going to stop helping him anyway, since I didn't appreciate having to drug myself so he could trash the living room. I only swallowed a little, a few bites, so that if you insisted on a blood test it would show. Way too much risk. The guy's a real loose cannon. It's too much stress for the money, so I was going to tell him I was out."

"But you didn't, did you?" Helena said.

"No." Phil squirmed. "You had us set up this whole plan to catch him on the road. I figured, you know, he'd be real grateful to me for filling him in. He paid me off and asked me to do one last thing before we parted ways, making an appearance on the dock to lure you away from the bunkhouse and leaving my car where he could get it. I agreed. It wasn't personal, just money."

Brayden knelt to stare him straight in the eye. "It was very personal to me and I will make sure you get the maximum sentence." He slammed the car door shut so hard the window rattled before he returned to the bunkhouse.

Quinn and Addie still knelt next to Charlie, who was now starting to stir. At least Terrence hadn't killed him. Surviving Terrence a second time was certainly a feat in itself. Addie struggled to her feet, took two unsteady steps toward Brayden and tried to speak... But nothing came out of her mouth. Her legs shook. Quinn grasped her under the forearm to steady her.

Time stood still in the tension that stretched between them. He'd give anything not to have to tell her the truth.

"Katie?" she whispered. "Did he tell you where she is?"

Brayden managed to get it out. "No. Phil said he doesn't know. Terrence didn't tell him that part of the plan."

"What?" It was no more than a whisper from Addie, soft, like a prayer. She searched his face, desperate for him to cut down the fear that had to be infecting her like a virus.

He swallowed, mouth dry, no comfort to give. "Phil was the diversion so Terrence could abduct her."

Helena drew close to him, expression dour. He could feel their sense of defeat that echoed his own. "We've got the BOLO out," she said grimly. "Roadblocks will be in place within fifteen minutes, but..." She paused. "Hunter didn't catch him. I'm going now to help."

Didn't catch him. Brayden's last thread of hope unraveled.

Helena held up a baggie. In it was the forget-me-not necklace, the one from Katie's mother, the one she never took off. "This was on the ground. I'll see if Luna can track Katie's scent from her being forced in the car, at least detect which direction Terrence turned on the main road."

Forget-me-not. His senses numbed.

A whine of sirens announced the paramedics. Quinn waved in the ambulance. The medics hurried to assess Charlie. He looked dazed and he tried to argue when they explained he was going to the hospital. "I'm okay. I want to stay with Addie."

Addie did not even supply her usual no-nonsense rebuttal. She held his hand and kept staring at Brayden, beseeching, until he had to look away.

They loaded Charlie onto a stretcher against his protests.

"I'll go with him," Addie said. "Unless…" She looked again at Brayden. "Is there anything I can do to help you get Katie back?"

He had to force out a reply in the face of her anguish. "We'll handle it and keep you posted," he gritted out. "I promise."

"I'll drive her to the hospital and stay there as long as I'm needed," Quinn assured him.

Brayden nodded. He hoped there was enough gratitude in his expression to show his thanks to Quinn, since he still did not trust himself to speak. Fury and fear swept through him in waves.

Quinn guided Addie toward the main house. She walked as if she was plowing through a dense drift of snow.

He was left standing there, Ella shaking off the water, as the ambulance rolled away. Helena started to crouch next to Luna, but instead she rose and put a tentative hand on his arm.

"I'm just going to say it because I know what you're thinking. This isn't your fault. There was no way you could have known that Phil was on the take." Then she opened the baggie and gave Luna a good whiff of the necklace and followed the wagging tail.

This is every bit my fault, he thought as he watched them track. He went back to the main house, which he knew in the next few hours would be turned into the center of operations for the flood of law enforcement that would descend upon the place to search for Katie. He would call the colonel from there. He surveyed the ranch once more, the sweep of autumn sun brushing the acres, the reindeer huddled together in the distant pens, the soft warbling of the river.

Addie's home. Katie's home. A sanctuary for the unwanted animals that had nowhere else to go. He would set the official wheels in motion.

And then he would personally tear up the acres one single inch at a time until he brought her home again.

Katie, I will find you.

From far away came the sounds and sensations, strange, unfamiliar, frightening.

Katie felt prickles under her chin as she swam toward consciousness. At first, she was too deeply lost in the dark to do anything more than acknowledge the sensation. Agony pounded her skull as she fought to wake up. Something terrible had happened. Fear circled around her, darting and biting without coming fully home to roost.

There had been pain. Terror.

Charlie unconscious.

And Terrence... Her eyes flew open, heartbeat zooming. She was lying on grass—not grass, *hay*, someplace gloomy and cold. Where was she? Fighting through the pain that pierced her skull, she got to her knees, where she realized her hands were no longer bound behind her. Her thighs trembled. Forcing her head up, she looked around. A barn… She was inside a barn. The hay strewn across the floor was dirty and clumped. How? She swam through her fractured recollections. The last thing she remembered was falling in the bunkhouse.

Charlie! Had he been badly hurt? Using a raggedy hay bale as a level, she pulled herself to her feet. Wobbling, she grabbed hold of the rough-hewn wall. Her vision blurred, then cleared.

Terrence had not left her to die. He'd brought her to this barn. Why?

The answer was obvious. He was delaying her murder in order to torture Addie. Anger slithered through the fear. *You're not going to hurt my aunt*, she silently promised. As long as she had one more breath in her body, she'd fight him with everything she had.

He'd given her time and she'd use it to plan her escape. As she sucked in some lungfuls of the dank air, trying to steady her breathing, she heard a soft clicking. She knew that sound.

She jerked a look around so fast it made sparks fly in front of her eyes. As her vision cleared, she saw the two reindeer, penned into a corner of the barn. Thunder had lost his antlers, but she recognized the big male right away. And next to him, Lulu, the sweet mother who had been separated from her tiny baby when

Terrence abducted both animals. Their agitated movements produced the clicking of their hooves. She half crawled, half staggered over to them.

"Hi, sweethearts." She put her hand through the slats to stroke Lulu. Tears threatened but she swallowed them down. "It's okay," she crooned nonsensically to the animals. "I'm going to get you out of here."

And how exactly was she going to do that? Brayden probably had no idea where Terrence had taken her. Thinking about Brayden and how he must be feeling fueled her resolve.

She stepped over a ruined saddle cast on the floor, walked over to the big barn doors and pushed at them. They swayed on their rusted hinges but did not give. Locked. Not surprising. There was no back exit. The only other way out was the enormous loft window some fifteen feet above her head. The ruined ladder indicated she would not be able to climb up there, even if she wanted to. The light that shone in told her it was probably late afternoon. How long had she lain there? A couple of hours? An entire day? And she had no clue where she was...

Her phone. She fumbled only to discover it gone. Of course Terrence would have taken it, or it was on the floor of the bunkhouse. Where was he right now? Had he stayed in the vicinity of the ranch, or driven for hours to spirit her away? She returned to the wall and found a missing knothole where she could see out. Crouching, she pressed her eye to the spot. There was a flat swath of dirt that vanished into a dense brushy area. A few scraggy trees poked through the low foliage, but it gave the impression of untended property that was isolated from any neighbors.

Katie felt a swell of desperation. "Now isn't the time to panic." A pile of soiled hay half concealed a car. Phil's security vehicle. She didn't know whether he was working for Terrence, or if perhaps Terrence had taken the vehicle by force. Whatever the case, there might be a way she could get the radio to work, or at the very least, find something she could use to defend herself.

She was about to go investigate when she caught the sound of the barn door slowly creaking open.

She swallowed down a scream as Terrence let himself in.

He wore the same faded jeans and long-sleeved sweatshirt. "Awake? Good. I was worried about freeing your hands, but it was too hard to lug you over my shoulder with them taped behind you."

She glared at him. "Did you kill Charlie?"

He shrugged. "Who knows?" He held up a chain and a manacle. "Look what I brought you. Jewelry."

Her muscles went limp. If he chained her, she would not be able to reach the car. The upside was it did not appear he wanted to kill her immediately. "Where is this place?"

"Old barn. That's all you need to know. Nice and cozy."

"You've made a mistake, kidnapping me. You should run. The police will be all over the area. They'll catch you."

He laughed, showing yellowed teeth. "Alaska is a great big place. They'll try their best, but they won't find this barn. It's all they can do to keep electricity going to this area." He jerked a thumb upward. "Gotta bring in the crews by helicopter to work on the lines because the roads are terrible."

Her spirit sank, but she was determined not to let him see her discouragement. "You're wrong. They'll find me."

He shrugged. "I'm only gonna keep you here a little while anyway, until I have a chance to touch base with Addie. She's going to give me the cash equivalent of what the ranch is worth."

Katie gaped. "She doesn't have that kind of

money. The ranch is mortgaged. You're wasting your time."

His lips thinned. "Then she'll fork over to me all she has and that will have to be enough for me. As long as she's ruined, I'll be happy. Maybe she can borrow from that doughboy with the mustache. I don't care. She'll pay until it hurts."

"And then you'll kill me anyway, won't you?"

His smile was wolfish. "Like I said, maximum pain." He moved closer.

Could she fight him off? She didn't think so. Her body was still trembling and she felt dizzy. Kick out at his knee. That worked last time. She shifted her weight.

"Sit down," he commanded. "I'm going to fasten this to your ankle."

"I won't."

He looked at her with eyes cold as Arctic snow. "I can knock you out with a shovel, if you'd rather. Then I don't have to listen to your yammering."

She sank down on the dirty hay. He fastened the iron manacle around her ankle and clamped the chain end to a metal rack that was probably used to hang harnesses and other equipment. He tugged on it to test the strength. "That should do."

"I'll scream," she said. "I'll keep on scream-ing so loud that someone will hear."

"Now, I'd like to see how long that would last. Go ahead. Scream the place down. There is no one to hear you." He bent so his face was closer to hers. "There is no one coming to save you. You are going to die in this barn, so if you want to spend your last few hours screaming until you're hoarse, go ahead. I think it will upset the reindeer, though." He laughed. "Then again, they're going to wind up dead here with you, depending on how long it takes them to find your body. Dumb animals. Useless, ex-cept for eating."

Chuckling to himself, he left the barn, slam-ming the doors shut behind him.

Even as she watched the dust settle to the floor, she knew she would not let him win.

Ever.

SEVENTEEN

Colonel Gallo came to direct operations for the search, along with several local cops and all the Alaska K-9 officers who could be spared. The tension was palpable; even the canines were subdued. Brayden pushed to be involved in every conceivable route. He and Ella drove the ranch property, combed the woods alongside Hunter and Juneau. Helena reported that Luna could not pick up a scent for Katie on the main road. She graciously offered to bring Addie home from the hospital along with Charlie, who had been checked over and cleared of major injuries by early afternoon. He managed to avoid Addie, who spent the rest of the day alternately sitting with Charlie or wandering through the house, listening in to see if there had been any progress.

There hadn't. The roadblocks had possibly been set up too late, or Terrence had headed off-road in Phil's vehicle. They'd found his

RV parked in the woods behind the ranch. It was being processed for evidence. The sheer enormity of the task was daunting. Alaska was 665,000 square miles of rough terrain, some of it nearly inaccessible. But Katie was out there somewhere, if Brayden could have only some slight indication of which direction Terrence might have headed.

When it was almost two, he was moving to his car again to start on the next search grid. He and Ella drove countless miles, his frustration mounting with each passing hour. Why hadn't Terrence been in contact?

To prolong the torture was the obvious answer.

"Brayden," Lorenza said, stopping him with his hand on the doorknob. "Take a break."

"Don't need one. I'm going out again."

She folded her arms across her chest. "You're tired. It's time to stop for a while."

"I'm all right."

"That's an order, not a suggestion," she snapped. Then she heaved a breath. "Look. Things went bad here. That happens in police work. I know how you're feeling."

"All respect, Colonel, I don't think you do."

Her shoulders stayed erect, but her face was creased with fatigue. "I love Katie like she was my own."

"I love her, too," he blurted.

The comment surprised her. She raised both eyebrows.

He should feel embarrassed, dismayed by his own admission, but he felt nothing but the burning desire to find her, to *save* her.

"I didn't know that's where things stood between you."

It doesn't, he should have said. *Just on my end.* But there was no point in bringing that up now. So he simply said, "I'm going to search. If you need to take my badge, do it. I'm going anyway."

"All right, Brayden," she said slowly. "This isn't the time to lose a good trooper. Do one more search route. Report back in an hour." She paused. "And you can keep your badge, by the way."

"Yes, ma'am."

He'd almost cleared the porch with Ella when Hunter called out. He'd been assigned to monitor any calls on Addie's cell phone. "It's Terrence," he said, covering the mouthpiece. "He wants to talk to Addie."

Brayden's hands itched to grab the phone and savage Terrence with all the anger that flashed through his nerves. Instead, he moved as close as he dared and waited.

"Just a minute. I'll get her," Hunter said to Terrence.

Addie was summoned. She took the phone with a quaking hand, poking the speaker button on. Brayden strained to hear every syllable.

"Where's Katie?" Addie demanded.

"With me. Still alive, unless you don't cooperate."

"What do you want?"

"Money. Five hundred thousand dollars should do."

Addie gaped. "I don't have that kind of money."

"Then you'll have to borrow it. I'll give you two days."

"And if I can't come up with it?" she asked.

"Aw, you know the answer to that. She dies, slowly and painfully."

Brayden's teeth ground together. Hunter scribbled a note and handed it to Addie.

"How do I know you haven't killed her already?" Addie said, prompted by Hunter's message. "I want to talk to her."

"No. You don't make the rules anymore. I do." A whirring sound caught Brayden's attention. A fan? He leaned closer and motioned for Addie to stretch out the conversation.

"Where…? I mean… How do I get you the money?" Addie said.

"I'll call you tomorrow and give you a bank account number. You'll transfer the money and I'll tell you where Katie is."

Again, the thwop of something spinning. A washing machine?

"Don't..." Addie whispered. "Don't hurt her, please. I'll give you anything you want. The ranch..."

"Nah. I heard that comes with a nice big mortgage. Too late. I want money. If you don't give it to me, she's dead. And tell all those cops if I see a sign of any of them she dies." The call clicked off.

"He has to be close," Hunter said. "I'll see if Eli can get a ping off a cell tower."

But Brayden was lost in thought.

"You have something?" the colonel said.

Brayden didn't answer. He had to think. He walked out onto the porch and stood there, letting the conversations whirl around his brain as he stared at the sun low on the horizon.

Terrence couldn't have gone too far. Somewhere isolated. But that could be a million places in the area. That whirring sound.

The whop of a rotor? He recalled Alex's remark.

"They're working on the electric lines and they have to drop crews in by helicopter. Noisy."

He leaped over Ella and ran back inside.

"The power company," he said. "We have to ask which lines they were working just now when Terrence called."

"What?"

"That noise in the background of the call. It's a helicopter crew working on the lines. There can't be too many crews out in this area at once."

The colonel was already on her phone. "I'll find out." Her question was clipped and urgent. When she disconnected, they stood staring at each other. Brayden willed Lorenza's phone to ring. It might be a goose chase, but he knew in his gut it wasn't.

It was the break he needed to find Katie.

It took five endless minutes before the answer came back. Colonel Gallo went to the map spread out on the table. "They have two crews working on the lines in this quadrant," she said, stabbing a finger at a spot on the map. "It's rugged terrain, which Phil's car would be hard-pressed to tackle, but there are three fire roads. Let's pull it up on Google Earth and see if there are any kinds of structures or landscape features where he could have hidden the car."

Helena tapped her laptop screen and zoomed in. "Fifty miles is a lot of area to cover," she said. Hunter and Brayden yanked out their laptops and each of them took different zones to search. He stared at that screen until his eyes burned. It was a whole lot of flat ground, blurred green and gray, without a farmhouse to be seen.

Could he have been wrong? *Again?* Had he sent them along a false trail in a direction that would take them farther away from rescuing Katie? Then it materialized in a small clearing, with one tiny adjustment of the mouse. An old, dilapidated barn. He zoomed in. It could be accessed from a fire road and was within ten miles of the spot where the electric crew was working on the line.

Lorenza was watching over his shoulder. "Is this it?"

"I don't know," he said, "but there's a solid chance."

"Go," she said. "And watch your backs. Terrence may be ready to deal with intruders."

Brayden ran for his car, along with Helena and Hunter.

Terrence might be on the lookout, but he had no idea what was in store for him.

And if he had already hurt Katie…

Brayden shut down the thought. He would follow his own advice and his mother's.

Eyes up, not down.

I'm coming for you, Katie. Hang on.

* * *

Katie pulled at the chain until the manacle cut into her ankle. The chain was not going to come loose from the wall, on that count she was certain. Only two choices remained—either she forced the iron band around her ankle to give way, or she got her foot out. The reindeer watched; in her mind they were quietly urging her on. The creeping shadows told her it was late afternoon, and her urgency increased. Escape in this nowhere spot would be exponentially harder when night fell.

A protruding nail in the barn wall finally came loose under her persistent wiggling. When it dropped into her hand, she immediately set about scraping at the rusted spot on the manacle. She worked until her nails were torn and bloody, but the iron held fast.

"Okay. Then we're going to go it the other way." She slipped off her shoe and sock. The cold air immediately numbed her toes. It was a matter of maneuvering, she told herself, just like easing a very large reindeer out of a very tight stall. With effort, she could point her toe and the manacle would slide clear to the bottom of her heel, and there it would stick. Try as she might, she could not get it to ease past that point. With a groan, she lay on her back, panting. If she didn't get free, Terrence would kill her. Even if she did, she might not make it out of the barn, but at least she wouldn't be a passive participant in her own destruction.

Shoving her hands into her jacket pockets, she tried to warm her fingers, which were stiff and cramped. Her fingers touched a tube of ChapStick. *ChapStick!* She sat up, uncapping the tube and slathering it on her heel until there was nothing left in the cylinder. Now she tried again, working the manacle lower and lower across the slippery ointment. Just when she thought she'd gone and permanently jammed the steel bracelet across her heel, the iron slipped free, taking some skin with it. Tears of relief gathered in her eyes. Tossing aside the manacle, she pulled on her shoes and ran to Phil's car.

The driver's door was unlocked. She eased it open, praying it did not squeak. The keys were tucked under the sun visor. She put them in her pocket. There was no radio affixed to the dash like in Brayden's car. The glove box? Nothing much in there but some paper and a stack of old napkins. She checked under the seats and throughout the vehicle, but there wasn't any weapon like she'd hoped, not even a can of pepper spray she might use against Terrence.

She popped the trunk and found a lug wrench. It wasn't the best alternative, since Terrence was strong, but it was better than nothing. She grabbed it. It was possible she could take him by surprise, hide while he was unlocking the barn door and wallop him. Then she'd drive the car for help and come back with a bunch of cops and a trailer for the reindeer. Brayden would be impressed.

What was he doing right now? She thought about the way she'd treated him, broken his heart. And he loved her. Or at least, he *had* before she lashed out at him. And now he was probably feeling tortured over his botched plan to catch Terrence.

Just what her demented uncle would want.

Well, Terrence was in for a surprise, because she wasn't planning on dying in this stinky barn. She would survive for herself, for Addie…and for Brayden. She owed him an apology.

And so much more.

The sudden bird squawk outside made her jump. Through the open loft window she heard it rocket into the sky and away. The reindeer reacted uneasily to the noise, too, eyes rolling as they shifted from hoof to hoof. Scooting to the knothole, she peeked out. At first, she saw nothing save the thick shrubbery.

Then there was the glint of something moving slowly along the fire trail. She pressed her face to the hole and tried to track it. A vehicle? Another glint. Two vehicles? Terror and hope warred inside her. She wanted to scream, but then Terrence would hurry to make sure she was dead before anyone came to her aid.

Uncertainty made sweat prickle her forehead. The minutes ticked by and she heard nothing but the pounding of her own pulse. And then there was another sound of movement, a crash from the wrecked farmhouse. With a flush of terror, she saw Terrence bash out the remaining glass from the front window as he aimed a rifle into the bushes.

Katie barely contained her scream.

"I see you," Terrence shouted. Then he let loose a volley of shots into the shrubbery. Katie clapped her palms to her ears. There was return fire and now she could see the top of a police car peeking out of the greenery. A dog barked somewhere, muffled. *Ella.*

Her breath caught. It was Brayden and Ella. Somehow they had found her. Elation and fear whirled inside her. Terrence had a good position from which to shoot, protected by the house and at a higher elevation than the police cars. Another blast from Terrence's rifle almost made her scream again. She had no doubt that he was well stocked with ammo and willing to keep shooting until the bitter end. Would he take the lives of Brayden? Hunter? Helena? Any of the other troopers who might be out there?

"Stop shooting," Brayden yelled. "Terrence, we've got you. Throw down your weapon."

Her pulse exploded at the sound of his voice.

"That's not going to happen," her uncle called out.

"Let Katie go and you'll get out of this alive."

"She's already shot, bleeding to death in the barn," Terrence sneered.

"No," she yelled. "He's lying." But there was so much shouting from outside and she wasn't sure anyone could hear her.

"Put down your weapon," Brayden commanded again.

Terrence fired another burst of gunfire. She had to do something to help. As she stood there, thoughts reeling, she noticed the weathered boards to the right of the big barn doors. They were fractured with cracks, warped and weakened by the elements. Weak enough? Only one way to find out. Racing back to Phil's car, she turned on the ignition and aimed the wheel straight for the moldy-looking board on one side of the swinging doors.

It was now or never.

EIGHTEEN

Brayden heard the revving engine one second before Phil's security car exploded through the barn door, showering bits of wood in its wake. Katie… It had to be. He charged from the cover of his vehicle, doing his best to stay concealed behind the shrubbery. If he could cut Terrence off before he took aim at the car…

But there wasn't time. Terrence turned his weapon onto Phil's front windshield, shooting repeatedly into the vehicle. Glass showered everywhere. He returned fire. The vehicle raced madly on until it smashed headlong into a rusted tractor, the front end crumpling. Terrence stumbled into view, ready to start firing again, when Ella exploded from the squad car barking so loudly that he jumped in surprise.

Brayden didn't stop to consider. He flat out sprinted after Ella and aimed a flying tackle that knocked Terrence flat. Hunter and Helena moved in. Helena kicked the rifle away and Hunter snapped on the handcuffs.

Brayden left the arrest and first aid to them. There was only one thought on his mind. He ran toward Phil's ruined vehicle. Terrence had fired directly into the driver's-side window. There would be no way he could have missed.

An agonized cry spilled out of him as he ran, skidding and slipping. Ella galloped after him. *Katie.* Reaching the vehicle, he yanked open the door.

His senses could not understand what he was seeing. The engine was still running, the accelerator weighted in place by a half-wrecked saddle.

No Katie, only a trick.

He spun around and charged for the barn just as she came running out. There was straw stuck in her hair and her face was slack with fear, eyes wild.

His heart leaped and spun at the sight of the dirty, disheveled, magnificent woman rushing toward him. He gathered her up in his arms and squeezed her tight. Ella ran over and danced up and down in excitement.

Thank You, God ran through his mind in an endless loop. In surprise, he realized he was saying the words aloud. She raised a trembling finger to his lips and quieted the stream of words. "I'm saying the same thing, that Terrence didn't hurt you." She shot a look around. "Any of you. We're all okay, aren't we?"

He simply could not speak until he swallowed hard. "Yes... We are."

She heaved in a breath. "Is Charlie alive?"

A question. He could answer and maybe get his body back online, though he could not remove his hands from around her. "Yes. He's going to recover."

She sniffed and sobbed, and he held on tight.

"She all right?" Hunter said, jogging over. "Ambulance is rolling."

"She's okay," Brayden affirmed, earning a smile from Hunter. He shot Helena a thumbs-up to where she stood guarding Terrence. Her wide grin shone clearly, even in the failing light.

Brayden stroked Katie's hair. "You figured sending Phil's car through the barn wall was the best course of action?"

She nodded, still sniffling. "Yes. It worked, didn't it?"

He smiled and resisted the urge to kiss her. Instead, he cupped her cheeks in wonder. "Yes, it certainly did."

"Guess what?" she said.

He stared adoringly at the woman before

him whom he loved with all his heart. "What?" he rasped.

"Thunder and Lulu are inside." Fat tears rolled down her face and she began to tremble harder.

Delayed shock, probably. "Let's get you to the car with a blanket around you."

She allowed him to guide her away from the filthy barn, Ella close by her side. "We can bring the reindeer home, back to the herd. Can you think of anything more wonderful than that?"

As a matter of fact, he could, but he wouldn't trouble her with it at the moment. "Addie will be thrilled." He sent a text to the colonel before he handed his cell phone to Katie.

"Tell her right now. I think it will be a call she won't forget."

It would certainly be a day he would remember until he drew his last breath on earth.

Terrence was in custody.

Katie was safe.

He closed his eyes and offered a proper prayer of heartfelt gratitude.

The following day was crammed with cleanup details. There was evidence to be painstakingly cataloged, reports to write, various online briefings to participate in. Brayden felt the spark of excitement in the K-9 team and in Colonel Gallo herself when he drove to Anchorage to have the official team debrief. Even Ella perked up when the cheer broke out that Terrence would stand trial for his crimes and the Christmas Fair would go on as planned.

"Got him," Gabriel said, pumping a fist. "One case down, two to go."

"And I've got some news to add on the Seaver investigation," Poppy said. "Remember the kid I talked to in the Chugach, the one I gave the note to? Well, I did some good old-fashioned legwork and I have some intel on him. His name's Xaviar Lemark. I don't have an address yet, but I'm getting closer. He's seventeen, same age as Harrison Seaver, Cole's son. When he talked to me, he said they were friends—at least, they used to be. And that Harrison is apparently unhappy living off the grid."

"Well, that's something to work on. Keep on it, Poppy," Lorenza said.

Brayden sensed a new energy circulating through the room. Another step forward on locating the Seavers for Eli's godmother. Maybe they'd catch a break on the whereabouts of Violet James, too. There was plenty more work ahead for the K-9 team and now he would be free to participate in the ongoing investigations. It was what he'd wanted, yet he felt as if his spirit still lingered behind at the Family K Reindeer Ranch.

He hadn't talked privately with Katie since the rescue, not properly, but when Colonel Gallo cleared her throat, he had a feeling he knew what was coming.

"And I'm sure some of you may have already guessed that our wonderful Katie Kapowski has tendered her resignation. She's decided to live with her aunt on the Family K full-time."

So she wouldn't be returning to her job with the Alaska K-9 Unit. He should be sad about it, but honestly, he couldn't picture Katie apart from the ranch, now that he'd seen her joy at tending to her precious reindeer family. It was where she belonged.

The meeting disbanded and he found his boss standing next to him in the empty room.

"Ready to get back to work, Ford?" she asked.

He hesitated. "I…uh… I think there's something I need to finish first at the ranch."

She cocked an eyebrow. "With Katie?"

He felt himself blush to the roots of his hair. "Yes, Colonel."

A savvy smile crept over her face. "Very good, Trooper. You go do that."

"Uh, ma'am? I'm not exactly sure that, you know, the whole thing will work out in my favor."

She stared intently. "Remember why I chose you for this case, Brayden? I wanted someone determined, averse to failure…"

He looked at his boots.

"With a touch of the goofball," she continued. "That's you to a tee."

"But…"

"You're dismissed, Trooper Ford. Go finish what you started." And then he was watching the door close, a plan forming in his mind.

In the early afternoon, Katie and Addie watched the herd as they greeted their long-lost members through the slatted wood. Thunder and Lulu had been given a quick vet exam and a clean bill of health, and it was time to reintroduce them to their family.

Katie unlatched the gate and allowed the herd to meander out, offering snuffled greetings. Tulip had revived enough to join them, too. Though she limped a good deal, she was welcomed by her new family. They might be three-hundred-plus-pound deer, designed with survival utmost on their priority lists, but it was clear as the ice crystals that formed on the morning pasture that these animals had missed their two abducted members.

And then Sweetie hopped along, bringing up the rear. He froze in surprise on gangly legs as he caught sight of Lulu. Katie clutched Addie's hand. Had the separation been too long for the baby to remember his mama? Sweetie twitched and trotted a few steps closer to Lulu. Katie realized she was holding her breath. Lulu shook her antlers and stretched out, bringing her velvety nose to rest on Sweetie's head. Her warm breath riffled his fur. And then he was snuggled up beside her and the two walked side by side to rejoin the herd.

Katie's face was damp with tears, as was Addie's. God had put everything right. There would be wounds to heal, residual memories to be dealt with, financial uncertainty ahead, but they *would* survive.

She hugged Addie gently so as not to aggravate her healing shoulder. "Will the volunteers come tonight?" Shirlene had shown up in person that morning with a plate of muffins and a report that the committee had reversed their vote.

"Not tonight," Addie said vaguely.

"Oh? I thought they were eager to get started."

"Well, tonight wasn't going to work."

"Why not?" Katie asked.

Her aunt shrugged. "Are you sure about this decision to leave your job?"

"Yes. Completely." She would miss her work with the K-9 unit, but she knew God wanted her here. "I want to thank Brayden before I go, though," she said softly. And there was a long-overdue apology she'd not been able to offer. Thinking of him made her heart squeeze uncomfortably, as if it was trying to beat with a missing piece. She reached up to fiddle with her forget-me-not necklace, only to be reminded that it was not there anymore. Another missing piece.

"Come on, honey," Addie said. "There's a pen to be cleaned. Let's start there, okay?"

"Yes, ma'am," she said.

They got to work. When they were finished, Quinn joined them.

Katie smiled at him. "I am so happy you've decided to stay on here. How could we run the place without you?"

Quinn ducked his head. "Aw, you'd manage. I like it here and my girls are going to love it on take-your-kids-to-work day," he joked, checking a message on his phone. "I was told to inform you that dinner will be ready in fifteen minutes."

"Dinner?" Katie frowned. "Who's the cook?"

But Quinn had already turned away.

"You go on and get a shower," Addie said. "You're a mess. We'll be right behind you."

Her suspicions prickled, but she followed directions. Clean and adorned in comfortably worn jeans and a long-sleeved T-shirt, she headed for the dining room thirty minutes later.

She was flabbergasted to find Brayden there, wearing the pink reindeer apron over his jeans and flannel shirt. His hair was newly cut, a mischievous smile playing around his mouth. Ella greeted her with a friendly bark.

Her pulse skittered at the sight of the handsome trooper who knew her better than anyone except maybe her aunt. "I didn't know you were coming."

He saluted her with a spatula. "That is because I am a master of stealth. I cooked dinner for us."

"You...*cooked*?"

He raised an offended eyebrow. "Don't sound so surprised. I can cook chicken and steak, and my pork ribs are..." He trailed off. "Okay, well, I haven't had much practice at the vegetarian options," he said, untying his apron and tossing it over a chair. He led her to the dining table and swept a hand toward a plate that held a peanut butter and jelly sandwich. It was cut into the shape of a reindeer, with pretzel antlers, raisin eyes and a bit of red grape for a nose.

She took it in, laughing in utter delight. "You made this for me?"

"Well, I made enough sandwiches for everyone, but you get the special reindeer version."

He pulled out her chair. "Would you care to sit, madam?"

She knew she could not let another second go by. Instead of sitting in the proffered chair, she turned to face him. "This is so special, absolutely sweet and perfect, but I can't enjoy a mouthful of it until I tell you something."

A look of trepidation crept across his features. "All right. I'm listening."

"I'm sorry, Brayden, so sorry about what I said to you before when I learned about the mortgage payment. I was upset, but it didn't give me the right to talk to you like I did. I've been thinking and praying about it, and you were right. I have used my independence as a way to keep people from me, but... I... I don't want it to keep me from you."

"Katie..." he started, but she cut him off.

"Please, Brayden. I have to finish. I'm sorry I hurt you. Those things I said, especially about Jamie, I wanted to justify my need to push you away. It was hurtful and unfair. I think... I mean..." She swallowed. "It hurt especially because... I love you."

Now his mouth opened in shock. She could not read the expression. Embarrassment? Reluctance?

"You love me?" he said hoarsely, as if the words felt strange on his tongue.

She wanted to run away, but there was no way to go past the awkwardness except to find a way through it. She swallowed hard. "I know things are different now, but I wanted to be honest and tell you that, since you were courageous enough to be straight with me. I don't expect you to return the feeling. But I hope we can be friends, in spite of everything. Can you forgive me?"

He blinked, as if he'd received a blow to the head. "Katie…"

"I get that we are probably not going to see each other much anymore, but I don't want things to end badly between us. Do you understand? I—"

"Yes," he said quickly. "I do. As a matter of fact, if you weren't such an interrupter, I was about to state my case." To her complete surprise, he dropped to his knee and opened a velvet box. Inside were two things: her forget-me-not necklace and a sparkling diamond solitaire engagement ring.

She went completely silent. "You were going to…to do this? Before I apologized?"

He smiled at her, the sweetest boyish smile she'd ever seen. "I love you, my darling Katie. I decided that I was going to go for broke and risk asking you even if you sent me packing. You're that special, that exceptional." His voice broke, and he cleared his throat. "And besides, I already asked Aunt Addie for your hand in marriage, and if I can get through her interrogation, I can handle anything."

Tears sprang to her eyes. "I can't believe it. I thought you were going to go back to Anchorage and I'd never see you again."

"I am going back to my job, of course, though I'll miss your gorgeous face at the office. At least I'll be able to go home to you every night, which should make up for things. Aside from my trooper duties, I think Ella and I are going to have plenty of time on weekends to come help out my wife's family outfit… *If* she says yes to marrying me, that is." He shifted uncomfortably. "And I hope she does soon, because my knee is starting to cramp up."

She realized he was still kneeling there, holding the box. "Yes," she said, eyes dripping with tears as he slid on the ring. "It will be the greatest honor of my life to be Mrs. Katie Ford."

"I love the sound of that." He got to his feet and swept her into an embrace, kissing her deeply. Ella added her bark to the excitement.

The kiss lasted until the applause broke out, and she pulled away to see Aunt Addie and Charlie holding hands, watching the proceedings. Both seemed to be grinning from ear to ear.

"He's kind of a klutz," Addie said, clearing

her throat, "but if I can tolerate Charlie, I suppose I can handle Brayden."

Charlie laughed. "A ringing endorsement. And speaking of rings, when are you going to accept mine, Addie? I'm going to keep asking until you say yes."

Addie rolled her eyes, but her cheeks were pink with pleasure. "Let's talk about it after the Christmas Fair. I have a lot to do."

"Anything you say, buttercup."

Addie waved him off, but not until he pressed a kiss to her cheek. "Let's leave these lovebirds to their plans."

Brayden smiled as they left. "Cute couple, aren't they?"

Katie laughed and kissed him. "Are you sure you want to trade in your relaxing weekends for work on this scruffy ranch?"

He looked at her with a smile full of love, and life and promises.

"I'm sure as eggs in April," he said, catching his bride-to-be in his arms.

* * * * *

*Look for the conclusion to the
Alaska K-9 Unit series,
Gabriel Runyon's story,* Blizzard Showdown
*by Shirlee McCoy,
as well as an Alaska K-9 Unit
novella collection,* Christmas K-9 Protectors
*by Lenora Worth and Maggie K. Black,
both available in December 2021.*

*Alaska K-9 Unit
These state troopers fight for justice with
the help of their brave canine partners.*

Alaskan Rescue *by Terri Reed*
Wilderness Defender *by Maggie K. Black*
Undercover Mission *by Sharon Dunn*
Tracking Stolen Secrets *by Laura Scott*
Deadly Cargo *by Jodie Bailey*
Arctic Witness *by Heather Woodhaven*
Yukon Justice *by Dana Mentink*
Blizzard Showdown *by Shirlee McCoy*
Christmas K-9 Protectors
by Lenora Worth and Maggie K. Black

Dear Reader,

Alaska, the last frontier. What an amazing place of breathtaking vistas and abundant wildlife. My husband (the darling Papa Bear) worked in Nome as a newly minted high school grad and he fell in love with the state, enjoying trips there with his family growing up. It was a blessing to be able to take our bear cubs there a few summers ago to revisit some of the places from Papa Bear's youth. Those memories are particularly sweet now that travel is curtailed for a while. Fortunately, I had the opportunity to interview Jane Atkinson, owner of the amazing Running Reindeer Ranch in Fairbanks. She was a wealth of information! You can see my interview with her on my Author Dana Mentink YouTube channel. I hope you enjoyed this installment of the Alaska K-9 series. As always, you can reach me through my website at www.danamentink.com or on Facebook and Instagram. God bless you all, my friends!

Dana Mentink